HOOVES OF THUNDER!

Twisting in the saddle for a quick look behind I found another smudge there—this undeniably dust. Swiveling round I found Bill Hazel's gaze locked in the same direction.

Edwardo came pelting back to swing his mount alongside Surefoot. "San Carlos Apaches!"

"How do you know?" I rasped at him, jolted.

"In here I know," he cried, thumping his chest. "No Navajos there—renegade Apaches ride under that dust!"

Probably took one Indian to recognize another. "Come on," I growled, "let's get these hides movin'."

With any luck, I thought, my own ponies bred for speed should be able to keep ahead of them. . . .

D0058938

Also by Nelson Nye

FIGHT AT FOUR CORNERS

NELSON NYE

BERKLEY BOOKS, NEW YORK

FIGHT AT FOUR CORNERS

A Berkley Book / published by arrangement with
the author

PRINTING HISTORY
Berkley edition / December 1992

ISBN: 0-425-13409-1

A BERKLEY BOOK ® TM 757,375
Berkley Books are published by The Berkley Publishing Group,
200 Madison Avenue, New York, New York 10016.
The name "BERKLEY" and the "B" logo
are trademarks belonging to Berkley Publishing Corporation.

PRINTED IN THE UNITED STATES OF AMERICA

10 9 8 7 6 5 4 3 2 1

CHAPTER
1

When I got the note from Terry O'Brian I was in the breaking pen topping off a handful of green-broke three-year-olds and didn't knock off to enter into any discussion. I knew without looking what the note would contain—a yelp for help—and my first reaction was to ignore it.

Reb Lockhart, the Circle Dot hand who'd come over with it, had left it on the top rail under a stone, got back on his horse and said with a jerk of the chin at the bronc I was forking, "Better you than me—too dang hot for that kinda work," and with a wave of a hand departed.

Common sense told me to stay the hell out of this. The Irish are a feisty bunch and this one, against all arguments, had bought present problems with both eyes open.

Trouble was that old loyalties, unlike old clothes, aren't kicked aside without second thoughts, and these brought back a whole flock of memories. We'd been close all three of us, Terry, Mark Elder, and myself, Gracious Gill.

Mark had always been the confident one, ever ready for a fight or a frolic, never once doubting he would have his own way. I was the uncertain, hesitant one, careful not to intrude or wind up with the lion's share. Even at the

1

occasional coyote or rabbit shoot Mark's gun would be out and banging away before I could get mine clear of leather. My only consolation came from hitting what I aimed at.

We'd gone to school together, shared childish pranks and enthusiasms, been practically inseparable until we'd grown up, and even then, going into the business of making a living, still felt we held a heap of views in common.

Then came the drought and a range in bad shape. Smallest holding was mine. With never near enough acres for cattle I'd gone in for horses, the expensive running kind, fed on oats and boughten bales.

The Circle Dot, Terrance O'Brian's spread and three times larger than mine, was back in the hills like my Lazy G—brush country with little grass and even less water.

Out on the flats where the grass was better with a couple of year-round streams and tanks fed by windmills were the three big outfits, Mark Elder's Bar B Cross, Ace Jolly's Tadpole and Diego Quintares' Rancho Villalobos, all three running cattle on the open range.

I had grown up an orphan, being raised by Mark's father, old D.J., who had treated me and Mark alike with the same disciplines and punishments, the same rewards for work well done. We'd always known Mark would inherit the ranch; I hadn't honestly expected anything, but when the time came for me to strike out on my own D.J. had loaned me the money—not yet all paid back—to set up a horse business on my eight hundred acres.

I owed old D.J., no question about it; but now that he was gone I was in the process of discovering son Mark to be not entirely like him. I'll not say Mark was a different breed of cat, but he certainly had ideas that did not jibe with mine. And the biggest difference that had so far surfaced had to do with Terrance O'Brian, a girl with ideas and convictions of her own.

She had lost her father two years ago, killed by a falling horse. Since that time she had managed to carry on with the aid of her father's three hands, but apparently it had been pretty uphill work. She wasn't one to complain, but eight months of drought had suddenly made her mind up and she'd sold off her cows and, despite everything I'd said on the subject, put the money into sheep. Which, in a country exclusively devoted to cows, was about as smart a piece of folly as attempting to rub your jaw with an elbow.

Peering into the future I could see nothing but trouble.

She had a lot of good arguments—but that's all they were, which didn't change anything. She couldn't stay with cattle in the face of this drought. Sheep were better foragers. They cost less than cows and could thrive in terrain where cows would starve. Took less hands to handle and could show more profit. I admitted these truths but had told her bluntly she could never get away with it, not around here. "These cow wallopers won't stand for it."

"It's none of their business what I do on land that belongs to me!"

"What help is that? You going to fence your land?"

She'd eyed me hotly. "I'd never be such a fool as to pour all my profits into barbed wire!"

"You think it's smart to run a renegade outfit? That's what it'll boil down to. These cowmen won't stand for it."

"These people are my friends," she'd said.

All I could say was, "I hope you're right."

It was noon before I picked up her note. Took me less than two seconds to read what she'd written: *Come over here to supper. I need your advice and have just taken your favorite pie from the oven.*

What good was my advice to a girl who wouldn't take it?

CHAPTER
2

Without I could manage to hang on to my temper I couldn't see any good coming out of going over there. You ever know a woman to admit she was wrong? Over the years I had learned that Terrance O'Brian could be as pig-headed as any female alive.

For more than half the afternoon I stewed and fumed over the prospect, knowing all the time that in the end I'd have to go. For the past year and more both Mark and myself had been courting her, him with all the advantages a big outfit could give a man. Naturally I wanted to go, to be near her even for a little while. Even if it provoked a blazing row. To ignore her invite could risk losing her by default, I thought. I had enough against me now.

Just like her, I reckoned, to have asked us both to supper!

I muttered and cussed till nearly three before I sponged the sweat off me, slicked back my hair and put on my Sunday-go-to-meeting duds. I threw a saddle on my night horse and finally, with a mort of misgivings, set off for the Circle Dot, four miles away as the crow flies.

Once I'd passed through my gate and shut it behind me the trail to the Circle Dot wound through the hills like a smuggler's track, mostly around them but sometimes over where the inclines were mere hogbacks. A pretty country, rough and wooded, dappled with shade and a heap of brush we could have done without, often hedging both sides like one was riding through a chute.

There were plenty of birds, the smaller ones warbling and twittering, cocking their heads at my horse as we passed. Now and again a family of grouse thundered into the air from right underfoot, as was their inevitable habit, causing old Surefoot to snort in feigned alarm.

At one spot the trail dipped close to the flats and forty feet of dug tank alongside one of Ace Jolly's windmills, where one of his crew on a horse with a rifle lifted a hand as we jogged on past. No threat, just a reminder of what this might come to if Terry persisted in her reckless defiance of cow country prejudice.

That cattle won't eat where sheep have browsed was an ingrained conviction that couldn't be shaken—an excuse to my notion. Another absurd fancy held that just the mere smell of them could turn cows from water.

I shook my head gloomily, knowing the cow crowd to be every bit as pig-headed as Terry O'Brian. You couldn't reason with them any more than with her. They weren't interested in facts, nary a one of them. I couldn't see where this would end but in disaster for all of us and—with the odds as they were—catastrophe for Terry unless she took the irrevocable step of importing gunslingers.

In this depressed mood, mind hemmed in by worries, I was in no hurry to arrive at my destination. Even less so at the likely picture of a confrontation with Mark when I got there. And in this uncomfortable hunch I was proved entirely right.

I saw his horse by the porch—verandah, Terry called it—soon as I got the house in my sights. He was sitting there

with her in the shade of the overhang chatting up a storm—
I mean literally, both of them looking about as friendly as
wet hens.

As I swung down I heard him say irascibly, "That's all
very well, but if you don't get those sheep out of here
there's going to be trouble, no two ways about it."

Ignoring him and his bellicose look she summoned a
smile to say with more seeming pleasure in my company
than I'd lately been able to notice, "How are you, Gracious?
You can hardly imagine how pleased I am that you were
able to get here."

That was one in the eye for Mark, I reckoned. Hat in hand
I climbed the three steps and dropped into a chair. "Mighty
kind of you to say so. I only just about did. This business
of raising market horses without any help but one Navajo
kid ain't the easiest way to make ends meet."

Mark, straightening his face, chipped in with, "It's certainly no way to get rich in a hurry."

I grinned back at him. "I don't expect to get rich. I'm
just tryin' to get by if it's possible." Eyeing Terry again I
said, "You're looking chipper."

That tugged a brief smile across her mouth. Getting
up she said, "If you boys can entertain yourselves a few
minutes I better go see how supper's coming," and slipped
into the house.

We looked at each other. "Stubborn as a dratted mule,"
Mark grumbled. "Whole country's in an uproar over these
sheep. I tried to talk to her mother—got nowhere at all.
They just don't realize how serious this is getting. Can't
you talk to her?"

"I said everything I could before she brought in the sheep.
It's her notion that long as the sheep remain on her property
she's as much right to have them as you and the other
owners have to run cows on the public range."

Mark smothered an oath. "We've always run cows on the public range—you know that. It's the way things are done, way they've always been done. Nobody's got enough ground under patent to stay in business more than two months if we didn't have use of what's outside our holdings. That's what free grass is all about. Way things are now with this goddamn drought we'd not last twenty days if we had to keep them up!"

I lifted my shoulders, let them drop with a sigh. "Where'd she sell her cattle?"

"Drove 'em in to that buyer at Four Corners," he growled. "Told her I'd take 'em if she was bound an' determined. But no, she wouldn't hear of it—independent as a hog on ice!"

By taking them to Four Corners, a two-by-four cowtown where the corners of four counties came together, she'd got them off her property without having to wait on someone else to do it, wanting I suspected to have done with it before word of her intentions kicked up a ruckus. Despite this reckless craziness she was no fool.

I'd seen by the arguments Terry had put up she'd not gone into this blindly—everything she'd said about sheep had been true; what she'd failed to grasp, what I'd been unable to get through to her, was the enormity, the damned outrageousness, of her decision. And now, I reckoned, appalled by the furor that decision had kicked up, she'd summoned us to help her find a way out.

She was in a real bind whichever way she jumped. With most of her money dumped into these critters, to get rid of them now at short notice could be ruinous. And hanging on to them in the face of the furious hostility their presence had aroused seemed practically certain to erupt into violence.

To Mark I said in a lowered voice, "As the biggest owner hereabouts, so long as she keeps them on Circle

Dot, couldn't you sort of talk down these hotheads—"

"Wouldn't do any good if I tried," he said angrily. "Thing has gone too far. The sheep are here. She's thumbed her nose at every cowman roundabout and, besides, she'll not keep them here—can't afford to. Sheep are like locusts, eatin' everything in sight! When they've stripped her range she's going to have to move them, and every one of these fellers knows it!"

I couldn't see any answer to that, for he was right. Sooner or later, regardless of good intentions, she'd have to watch them starve or move them onto new ground. This was the situation we were faced with in a nutshell.

"If you were her husband," I said with great reluctance, "you—"

His snort of expelled breath cut me off. "I already thought of that; she won't have me on those terms. Bowed up like a carbuncle! Said it would look like admittin' she was wrong, which she wasn't. Said an O'Brian didn't back down for anyone, me included!"

Terry's supper turned out to butter no parsnips, a most uncomfortable affair for everyone involved. Not even her mother's talking talents, which were considerable and artfully employed, were able to bridge the constraint imposed by the angry resentment locked behind the faces of Mark Elder and the girl. Nor was I much help with a mind filled with pictures of bloodshed and strife.

Mark left early with the barest of apologies, pleading a previous engagement.

Mrs. O'Brian, who all along to my notion had been favoring Mark's suit, retired to the kitchen saying she'd take care of the dishes.

"Let's sit on the verandah," Terry said, shooing me ahead of her. We sat and looked at each other for I don't know how long. Finally she said with the blunt directness that could be so devastating, "Damn those pig-headed mule-stubborn cow wallopers!"

"Damn 'em all you want. Won't change anything."

"But it's so unfair!" she cried resentfully. The moon was up, blackening the shadows, turning the porch near as bright as day. I could see angry color in the slant of her cheeks. "All I want is to be left alone—"

"Then you ought to be pleased," I said gruffly, grinning. "Far as those sheep are concerned you're plumb alone, no getting around that. I did my best to tell you how it would be."

"But they're on my own land, they're not bothering anyone!"

"You'd better face facts, girl. They're botherin' everyone and you damn well know it. And when they're bothered enough you're going to be in bad trouble, and you know that, too."

"If that's all you've got to say you might as well go home!"

Discarding her customary boots and jeans she had got herself into a dress for the occasion—a real concession on her part; she had her hair up becomingly and, had she let herself relax, you might have taken her for a lady instead of the hoydenish half boy her father's need and her own inclinations had made of her.

I broke through the piled-up silence to say, "You made a first-rate hand with cows on this spread, but you're never going to make it with sheep, believe me. These cow wallopers ain't goin' to let you."

She stared at me in a distracted way. "There must be something I can do to change their minds." With those green eyes probing my face she said, "According to Mark the only choice I've got is to marry him."

"Well," I said, "what's so wrong about that? It's what your father and his both wanted, isn't it?"

"Marry him and these sheep will be gone like a June frost! That's no solution. I've always wanted to leave a mark on this country. I—"

"You're in a good way to realizing that," I said with a piece of a grin on my face. "The girl who fetched sheep to the Four Corners country! That will sure as hell place you in local history."

Her laugh was brief and angrily bitter. "You're as bad as Mark. You think all a girl is good for is babies!"

"Well, they're sure fine for that," I said brightly.

All that fetched was a curl of the lip. "I wish you'd be serious."

"You could always marry me," I said.

"Yes, I know. A typical man's response." Her face came around to look up into mine. "I don't want to be shut away in a house. I want to *do* things, *be* someone!" she cried rebelliously. "Oh, how am I going to get out of this fix? Without, I mean, giving up my sheep. That I *won't* do."

"If you don't you're likely to get them killed."

"If those sheep are killed I'm going to kill me some cows!"

"Salty as Lot's wife. Look," I said, "these cowmen ain't foolin'. You want to wake up in a coffin?"

"There must be some way I can protect them."

"Sure," I said, "but it'll cost you. You can bring in some hired guns and really stir up this hornets' nest."

I could see straight off I'd been a fool to say that. Evidently it was something she hadn't yet thought of and I could see she was interested. "Damnation," I said, "that'll really kick the lid off!"

"A man's home is his castle. I've just as much right to protect *my* property!"

"Good night," I growled, getting out of my chair. "I can see you're not ready for any worthwhile advice."

I was halfway to the gate and my ground-hitched horse when she caught hold of my arm. "You're the only true friend I've got anymore. Don't go off like that—can't we be like we used to? Can't you smile for me, Gracious?"

"What you've got yourself into is no smilin' matter."

"I know," she said meekly. "I can't think where to turn if you give up on me."

She walked with me to the gate. "I'm not giving up on you. It's just that—"

"I know," she said softly, and abruptly turned stiff as a cigar-store Indian. "What's that?" she cried, staring.

Following those widened eyes, I said, "Looks like paper."

And that was just what it was, a folded bit of paper under a stone on the gate's crosspiece. Terry pushed off the stone and picked up the paper. The moon was bright, but not bright enough to read by. I struck a match on my pants leg and looked over her shoulder. It was plain enough now.

Get rid of those sheep or we'll do it for you.

CHAPTER
3

"That does it!" cried Terry, looking vengeful as a stepped-on rattler. "Where do I look for these hired guns?"

"You don't," I said. "It's surefire suicide to go that route—"

"Don't think I'm going to stand by while they slaughter my sheep and not lift a finger! If they're going to start killing I'll give them a bellyful."

"Not with my help," I told her flat out. "You put gunslingers on the Circle Dot payroll they'll start hirin' the same kind of trash and first thing you know we'll be neck deep in a range war you can't win! Protectin' your sheep is one thing; you don't need gunfighters for that. All you need's a few hard-noses that understand sheep and won't be scared off."

"All right. Where do I get them?" She still looked fierce but her voice was more reasonable, so I reluctantly said, "There's a kind of customer of mine, a sort of amateur bandit . . . sticks up a few stages when he runs short of cash. Used to be in the sheep business himself till he got run out. Might be he could help you . . . it's just an idea."

"If," she said, eyeing me curiously, "he got run out of the sheep business, I don't see where he could be of much help to me."

"Pretty versatile gent, learned a few things before they got done with him. Kind of an uncle to Edwardo, kid who works for me. Ride over in the morning and you can speak your piece."

Watching me closely she said, "Ride over where?"

I should have known better, all things considered; fact is I did but couldn't resist the look in those eyes. Not pleading exactly . . . it went deeper than that.

She said again, "Ride over where?"

"My place."

"What makes you think he'll help me?"

"Kind of a two-way street. Piki's my best customer . . . bought six or eight horses in the past several months. Think he'll do it to oblige me."

Her face lighted up. She caught hold of my arm again, leaning toward me, excited. "You're going to help— you're—you're throwing in with me?"

"Let's just say I'm not bucking you."

Though her smile dimmed noticeably it was still in evidence. She squeezed my arm. "I'll be there," she said.

The moon was pretty well down, sliding toward the far horizon, deepening the shadows as I came into my yard, my glance flicking around in the pride of ownership. There wasn't a great deal to see. Low four-room house, forge shop and long stout barn with stalls for the horses I wanted to keep up. It had cost me a bundle to fence eight hundred acres—and not all paid for yet—but with the kind of stock I had gone in for no one but a plumb idiot would have turned them loose on the open range. Gamblers' horses ain't to be found back of every bush. You could buy cow horses for forty dollars a head. It took a hundred such to pay for one of mine.

I didn't have a bunkhouse; kid slept in the barn. I cooked for both of us. There were two strong corrals, one of them a day pen, both built of mesquite posts and rails, each joint lashed with strips of green hide. I unsaddled, turned Surefoot into the day pen and put up the bars. Took a look in the barn, heard the kid snoring and went into the house.

Satisfied I'd had no intruders I pulled off my clothes and got into bed. But there was too much on my mind to drift straight off into sleep. Reckoned I'd been sort of reckless to have stuck my neck out far as I had with that offer of help . . . word might get around but it made, I thought, a kind of satisfying contrast to the amount of help she was getting from Mark.

And after all, she did have a right to protect her own property.

While it was still dark next morning I sent Edwardo off to fetch his uncle, the elusive Piki Barbona.

Terry O'Brian was the first to arrive. She rode into the yard a bit before ten and we sat down on my porch to pass the time while we waited, leaving the horse I had given her on trailing reins and a loosened cinch.

"Is this fellow you mentioned likely to be arrested?"

"Don't believe so," I said. "Learned a good while ago not to be careless. Takes off nothing but cash, never touches the mail. Most folks round and about don't have a heap of use for Wells Fargo, think they're high chargers. Some of them probably know about Piki, but so far at least they've kept their mouths shut."

"Who's shipping cash?"

"Banks mostly—payrolls for the mines."

Edwardo rode in some half hour later with the man we were waiting on.

Piki Barbona, who had grown up in Mexico, was a big solid man with the beginnings of a paunch hanging over his belt. He wore a huge black mustache beneath his dust-colored sombrero, a gun hung from his hip and there were crossed bandoleers well stuffed with rifle fodder across his broad chest. He swept off his large hat with an elegant flourish when I introduced them and the laugh wrinkles showed around his twinkling blue eyes. "I am honored," he said with a grin, and we got down to business.

Terry had told him her problems, explaining what she was up against, and Piki nodded, very sympatico. "Five hombres and myself," he assured her, "should be enough to take care of this."

"How much?" she asked nervously.

"Oh, for you," he said brightly, "ten dollars a day, plus the ammo."

Her glance jumped to me. "I'll take care of the cartridges," I said. "Cause less comment than if you bought them yourself." And, to Barbona I said, "Forty-five nineties?"

He nodded.

"Understand," I said, "if there's trouble it's all right to knock the legs out from under them—bust up an arm, but no killing. Savvy?"

"Sure," he said easily and, turning back to the girl, told her, "we'll be at your place before dark." He swung a leg over his saddle and took off.

She said to me, still looking a bit dubious, "Do you suppose this will work?"

"It'll hold them off for a while anyway. When they see you mean business they'll have to rethink their notions. These boys are fighters and won't be caught napping."

She gave me a contemplative look.

Taking a guess at her thoughts I said, "If you run short of cash let me know and I'll take care of it. Fighting wages come high, but you'll not lose many sheep with him around. Rest easy. I'm off now for Chandler."

During the long ride to Chandler I had plenty of time to sort out and hash over the considerable damage so easily done by a well-meaning friend. Initially, after reading that note we had found on her gate, my gab had been directed at getting the frozen look off her face, easing the impact of what she'd got herself into. And yes, of course, helping myself stack up better in her mind than Mark.

That perhaps had been more excusable had I not compounded my folly by bringing that irresponsible cowman-hating bandido, Piki Barbona, and his trigger-happy renegade hellions into this. And now here I was sneaking over to Chandler to fetch them the means of raising hell and shoving a chunk under it.

Honestly aghast at my role of aiding and abetting what could well turn into a full-fledged range war—the very thing I'd sought to avoid—I berated myself for ever opening my mouth. Small comfort could I offer should my introduction of that notorious blood-letter prove the cornerstone of her undoing.

My cautioning of Barbona and his too-ready acceptance of the terms of his employment would restrain that hombre not in the least once the guns started banging. He had old scores to settle against anyone making their living from cattle. Too well had I known his feelings on the subject of cowmen; so why had I gone out of my way to fix it up for her to hire him?

A man doesn't care to delve too deeply into things he feels ought to go against the grain. It was in no comfortable frame of mind that in Chandler I invested in an entire case of .45-90s and, with this divided into sacks for easier carrying, presently got on my horse and set out for home.

The evening's darkening shadows stretched long before me as I climbed into the hills that would take me to my eight hundred acres. Who, after all, aside from Terry, would be likely to know my part in this feud? And Terry, of course, wouldn't think of it that way.

Putting my deviousness aside in the reach for something better to think on I cantered into the yard to find Barbona waiting.

CHAPTER
4

As promised he had fetched five sheepmen with him. Black
Yaquis these were, big brawny devils in Chihuahua hats and
crossed bandoleers, Colt .45s joggling their thighs and a
plain burning hunger to line their sights on a cowman, each
with a Winchester tucked under his left leg.

He got up off the steps to throw an arm round my
shoulder. "Relax, amigo. With Barbona on the job there
is no cause for worry. We know about these things. We
know how to handle them."

"Yes, well, just remember what I told you—no killing. If
there has to be killing you be sure these boys don't start it."

Barbona grinned, but not in a way you'd care to write
home about. "If one of my Indios is killed by them bastards, I will kill two of them—two of them for every Indio
that dies!"

"Just be sure they kill first. That way," I told him, "our
side's in the clear."

His grin wasn't the sort that carries conviction. "Where
is this place of the sheep?"

He thought he was dealing with a dumb cluck I reckoned,
but my boots were clean; he'd had his warning. Whatever

he did now was out of my hands. I gave him directions and he said, "Where's that ammo, you got it in them sacks?"

"Sure. A sack for each of you." I passed them over and he parceled them out.

"Adios, amigo," he offered with the lift of a hand; *"Vaya con Dios,"* I called after them as the horses I'd sold him went up the trail that wound through the hills toward the Circle Dot.

I went back to my work of readying horses for sale.

Several days slid past without untoward happenings. And then one morning as I came out of the house I spied Ace Jolly coming through the gate, my nearest big neighbor and one who'd put up twenty windmills to feed dug tanks on public land. An important man hereabouts and, despite his name, an encroaching sort.

He looked anything but jolly as he came into the yard and stopped his horse some twenty feet from me to crook a leg about the horn. His mean little eyes went over me sharply from hat to boots and back up to my face. "You hear about O'Brian putting on more help?"

"How's that?" I said, reaching deep for surprise.

"One of my hands happened to ride past her spread. Says he saw a couple big-hatted Yaquis with dogs handlin' sheep, an' ten minutes later he spotted three more. What the hell is she up to?"

"Maybe her three punchers didn't like herdin' sheep. You reckon they've quit?"

"Ain't heard nothin' about it. Them Injuns Pete saw was all packin' Winchesters. Didn't look, he says, like the kind that generally traipse after woollies."

"Way you fellers been talkin'," I said, "might have put her wind up. I did hear somebody left her a note saying if she didn't get rid of her sheep they'd be got rid of for her. After all, Ace, she was brought up to believe she had some rights in this community—"

"She hadn't no right to bring in sheep!" he snarled, looking ugly. "Nor rifle-packin' Yaquis! By Gawd, we ain't goin' to stand for it!"

"Have you talked to Mark Elder?"

"Damn young fool makes no more sense than a busted flush! Alls he can think about is gettin' her to bed!"

"Don't hardly seem like molesting her sheep would improve his chances much."

He eyed me a while like he was debating something. "Whose side are you on?"

"I'm in no position to take sides, but I'll say this much: You can catch more flies with honey than by swattin' at them. If she's importing Yaquis it's because she's been threatened. If I was you I'd leave her alone. She'll probably have to get rid of them anyway once the critters have eaten up what graze she's got left."

He looked like that notion hadn't occurred to him. Then something else appeared to catch his notice. "Seems like I've heard you been after her too." He studied me suspiciously.

"Sure. I'd hoped at one time I might put my brand on her, but stacked up against Elder and his Bar B Cross I've about as much chance as a snowball in hell."

He wasn't interested in me. He said with a snort, "You can tell her for me them sheep's got to go. Them Yaquis won't save 'em—go tell her that!"

"I got better things to do with my time," I said flatly. "If you want to make fighting talk tell her yourself."

His look turned nasty and he said like Moses handing down the Ten Commandments, "You stay outa this—hear me?"

A piece of my temper came up like bile and it took real effort to keep hot words penned back of my teeth. When he saw I wasn't about to talk back at him he spun his horse and went larruping off.

It was hotheads like him that made bad situations worse, and if Mark didn't balk it was dollars to doughnuts there'd be a deal of shooting before this ruckus was finally ironed out.

Barbona was tough and plenty seasoned with experience, but that he could hold back these sheep haters I didn't believe. If they were bound and determined there was one thing he could do and this was to make their intentions expensive. They'd both money and numbers and I could see no way out of what was shaping up.

I wanted mightily to help her but all my stewing and cussing only left me more frustrated and produced no plan that could do more than prolong what seemed certain to wind up as a bloody disaster.

It was three days later while we were working with the horses that Edwardo looked up and said company was coming. Turned out to be some fellow I had never seen before. He pulled up outside the corral and said straightaway that he was in the market for a fast horse. By his garb I reckoned him either a gambler or a preacher. I didn't think he looked genial enough to be any sky pilot.

He didn't have no hair on his face. He had a cold jaw and a pair of eyes you couldn't read, one of which stared straight ahead while the other took in everything there was to see.

"All I've got is fast horses."

"But some, natural enough, is faster than others."

"I suppose so," I said. "Just what sort are you looking for?"

"One that'll outrun a posse." He fixed the good eye on me. "Pick out one that'll get me to Texas."

"I don't pick them out; that's up to the customer."

That good eye scrutinized my face for a while. I said, "Reckon you're not wanting any green-broke horse."

"That's right. What's the tariff?"

I said, "You can pick any horse I've got on the place, including those in the barn. Makes no difference to me which you take. I'm a one-price man. These nags sell for five hundred a head."

"What are they, solid mahogany?" A sneery smile crossed the edge of his mouth. "You won't sell many at that price."

"Sell enough to keep beans in the pot."

He stared awhile longer. Got out of the saddle. "I'll have me a look at those in the barn."

"Help yourself," I said.

He came back after a spell with a halter and leadshank on a short-coupled four-year-old gelding about the color of sand. He knew horses all right. Dropping the shank he stepped over to the horse that had brought him and hauled a fat roll of bills from the saddlebag nearest and peeled off five C notes. "Don't get no ideas. I'm a dead shot," he said.

"What I figured," I told him, accepting his money.

He got the saddle and bags off the old horse and settled them on the new; took off the halter and put on his bridle. With his new purchase ready for the road he put the halter on the other one and climbed into the saddle. "So long," he said and rode off, the haltered horse cantering alongside.

"What'd you make of him?" I asked Edwardo.

"Won't no grass grow under that feller."

Seemed like this was my day for visitors. Not much more than an hour had passed when Mark Elder rode into the yard. I put a leg over a bar and ducked under another, then walked over and invited him to get down and stretch. When all that fetched was a grunt, I said, "Got time to set a spell?"

"On my way to see Terry. Guess you know about her hirin' them Yaquis?"

"Ace was here bellyaching about it."

"You know that damn Mex outlaw is over there?"

"Who's that?"

"That sheepman they ran out of Showlow—Piki Barbona."

I whistled. Then I said, looking into his angry stare, "Can't hardly blame her, way you fellows been throwin' threats around."

"She'll have to get rid of him. Hirin' that feller's a goddamn outrage! We're not going to stand for it."

"Better not put it to her in that fashion. She ain't in no mood to be pushed around."

"No one's pushing her around. How about riding over there with me?"

"You mean to talk sense at her?"

"By God, somebody's got to do it!"

"Well, don't count on me."

"What's that supposed to mean?"

"Means just what you think it does."

"Sometimes, by God, I don't understand you!"

"Likewise," I said. "For a fellow that's spent as much time as you have tryin' to talk her into marriage, seems to me you ain't using your head. You know well as I do why she went into sheep. Simple matter of survival. Now you want her to get rid of the only cash crop she can raise on that place."

"She can't raise sheep in cow country!"

"If that's what you believe why not give her a chance to find it out for herself?"

"Once they've stripped the Circle Dot she's going to have to move them—"

"Ain't stripped it yet," I said mildly.

"Just a question of time and you know it!" Glaring angrily he said, "Then she'll have them Yaquis shove them onto the open range."

"To which she's just as much right as you have." I held up a hand. "What does Quintares say about it?"

"I ain't asked him, but he'll side with us of course. Why wouldn't he?"

"Don't know. Just wondering is all. Has it never occurred to you he might be wanting to marry her himself? Part of his range butts up against hers. He might surprise you. Always kind of figured him a dark horse myself."

CHAPTER
5

I'd been glad of the chance to shove a spoke in their wheel, a bit of grit in the machinery of those cow barons who looked on this range as their own private stomping ground and expected all hands to jump when they yelled "frog." Anything I could come up with that might get them squabbling among themselves wouldn't hurt Terry's chances and might in the long run improve them. A little.

Even a little was almost more than a man could honestly hope for, considering the odds stacked against her. Sheep on the whole are pretty stupid critters and easily panicked. She'd enough on her plate without any outside harassment.

Though I'd fetched Barbona and his Yaquis into this to give the cow crowd something to think about and Terry some teeth to bite back with, I was being chafed now by a fattening fear that their presence might not only militate against her but bring on the very clash I'd been trying to postpone. Barbona, chock-full of hate as I knew him to be, might prove a damn poor reed to lean on—no better in fact than a stick of thawed dynamite. Entirely unpredictable.

As the days dragged along the specter of defeat continued to haunt me along with a worsening depression, which sprang from knowing myself impotent to prevent what figured to be a nearing disaster, not only to Terry's own private dreams but to the whole future of this Four Corners country.

The shortness of tempers brought on by this drought combined with that overriding prejudice against sheep needed but a single unjustified act of violence to plunge us into a bloody range feud very likely to be on a par with the Pleasant Valley war. It was a sickening prospect and no mistake.

The Circle Dot, to my thinking, was headed for oblivion. The only possible chance I could see for saving it was to split up the cow crowd by whatever means could be fetched to hand. Some sort of distraction was direly needed, a damn bad fright, or something that would provoke distrust among them. But what and how to devise it played hell with my sleep for many a night.

I considered a brush fire, but all of the brush was up here in the hills. More sheep seemed an answer, but where would I get them? And how control them? I might use Barbona, but the result might prove worse than the mess shaping up already. I thought of paying a visit to Diego Quintares, the third big cattleman in this region, but discarded the notion.

If I could dredge up something and make it seem plausible, Ace Jolly was the bugger to work on. If I could locate that hardcase who'd just bought a horse from me . . . but I'd no idea where the hell he had got to. He was probably in Texas by this time.

If a range war erupted in this Four Corners country there would be easy pickings for some unscrupulous outsider; though it wasn't a question of if but of when. Easy pickings was a surefire invitation to the buzzards and vultures who fattened on violence. But if I could come up with some way of maneuvering the bastard I would have in Ace Jolly the means right at hand. Of the three biggest cowmen Jolly was the one who had the least range at present. A born conniver, greedy and suspicious by nature, ever ready to believe somebody was trying to get their knife in him . . . a hard-nosed hog who'd be easily persuaded.

That, anyway, was how I saw him.

The hell of it was I could not in good conscience sic him on Mark. Mark's old man had done too much for me, so it would have to be Quintares. I had nothing whatever against Quintares but, as a Mexican, he'd be a natural object of suspicion to a man of Ace's caliber. A few well-chosen words ought to prod Ace Jolly into something unforgivable.

In the local pecking order Quintares was second only to Elder, in range and crew size and everything else. If Ace could be persuaded that Quintares had visions of becoming top dog in this Four Corners country and aimed to use Ace's share of the public domain as the stepping stone . . .

Having let these thoughts simmer for a couple of days, on the third I rode over to pay Ace a visit.

Tadpole headquarters was an unkempt assortment of jerry-built structures for the most part held together with baling wire. I found Ace sitting on his ramshackle porch with a jug of white lightning on a table at his elbow. No one else was in sight. Ace wasn't the sort to waste his cash on idle hands. "Git down," he grunted, tipping back the jug.

He set it down with a belch and dragged a hand across his jowls. "What's on your mind?"

"Just wondering," I said, "if you had any idea what Quintares is up to."

"What do you mean up to?"

"Been looking over those tanks and windmills you've been scatterin' over your share of the public range. Sort of wondered if he was figuring to buy you out."

Ace straightened up to stare at me, scowling. "First I've heard of it."

"Maybe you ain't heard he's been hirin' more hands?"

"Hell, he's got ten men ridin' for him now. What's he want with any more?"

"Don't know . . . unless it's tied in with . . . Someone was saying he's a changed man since he's been courtin' the O'Brian—you heard anything about that?"

Jolly's mean little eyes jumped at me like poisoned darts. *"Terrance* O'Brian? I don't believe it!" He was off his behind now, fists clenched, glaring. "She wouldn't marry no Mex'kin!"

"Pretty hard thing to swallow, ain't it? But she might, you know, if he was top dog and would let her keep those sheep an' all." I nodded as if to some notion inside of me. "Might tie in with those new hands he's takin' on."

Ace's face was a study, shaved-hog jowls gone the color of leaf lard mixed with dust and his eyes, what could be seen of them, shining like two pieces of black glass.

"Understand," I said, "this is only a rumor I thought you might know something about. Fellow stopped by to get him a fast horse. Give out Quintares told a friend of his he was about to take over another piece of range and was puttin' on men to handle it."

"By Gawd," Ace growled, "I'm goin' to look into this!"

I said, "There ain't but three places he could have in mind. Yours, mine or the Circle Dot, and I sure can't see Terry selling hers." I gave that a moment to sink in before saying, "Figured he must've made you an offer."

"Well, he ain't," Ace declared like he'd a mouthful of grit.

"It's possible, of course, he ain't figurin' to *buy*. If he's puttin' on more hands he might have something else in mind."

"Yeah . . ." Ace said, and I got back on my horse. I said, looking worried, "He's just about big enough to gobble the both of us."

CHAPTER
6

With a fellow like Ace there was no telling what he'd do with all this stuff juning round in his head. He could go charging over to Quintares' headquarters like a rampaging bull to confront the man. I didn't think he would, but as I saw it he'd be too filled with notions either way to bother about Terry's sheep for a while.

I thought of riding over to chew the rag with Mark at the Bar B Cross, but in the end I judged it smarter to drop a few bugs in Quintares' ear.

The Rancho Villalobos was what Quintares called his spread. Red tiled roofs and a bell tower sat above a cluster of smaller adobes, all of them gathered round the main house gussied up with whitewash, the whole surrounded by a stout eight-foot wall; the man lived I thought like a feudal baron in the midst of this irrigated greenery of cultivated fields and orchards worked by his peons and innumerable relations.

As I rode up to the gate one of his peons pulled it open and bowed me through, and I went on to pull up before the tree-shaded gallery that fronted the whole length of the house. There a man in cotton pantalones invited me to get down, and would have led away my horse had I been of a mind to allow this. "Don Diego?" I inquired, and a servant stepped out to hold wide the door. "Come in, señor," called a voice from beyond it, and Quintares himself escorted me into his comfortable living room, clapped his hands and ordered refreshments.

He was a slim man of medium height dressed in charro clothes and appeared to be in his middle forties. A rather distinguished looking gent with a Spanish cast of countenance. I'd never been here before and had seen him only from a distance.

"Welcome to Rancho Villalobos." He smiled, inclining his head as a *moza* came in with wine and little cakes on a tray, which she placed on the small table nearest us. Don Diego poured us each a glass. "Your health, señor."

I took a couple of small sips and he invited me to sit down.

Ensconced in a comfortable chair I watched him pull up another to sit facing me, brows raised in polite inquiry.

What I had in mind was easier thought of than broached in the face of such genial hospitality. "My name is Gill. You've likely heard me mentioned. I breed running horses."

He inclined his head. "Very good ones, I'm told. Have you come to talk about them?"

"Not really. I thought perhaps you should know there's a rumor afoot that you've been hiring more men and have intentions of expanding your operation, presumably by purchasing or seizing more range. Is there any truth to this?"

"I can assure you there is not," he said gravely.

"Then it's only fair to tell you some of your neighbors— one, anyway—is taking this gossip pretty seriously. Another piece of gossip links you with the Tadpole and the Bar B Cross in a determination to be rid of those sheep the O'Brian girl has fetched into this country. I don't imagine you're one to make war on a woman."

"Certainly not." He considered me a moment. He drew a hand over his face and eyed me some more. I couldn't read what thoughts were behind those dark eyes and rather wished I'd not ridden over here.

"I don't suppose," he said, "you'd care to put a name to the man who imagines I covet his range?"

I shook my head. "When it's discovered you have no such intention it will probably blow over."

Quintares nodded. "Let us hope so. I have no desire to become embroiled in a feud over land or anything else. How are you making out with horses?"

"I manage to keep a few beans in the pot. Not everyone cares to put money into high-priced nags. I'd have done better I suppose to have gone into roping and cutting horses. We've a pretty fair market around here for those."

"Has this drought hurt you much?"

"Well, it's forced me to buy feed. A lot more than I'd aimed to."

"If I may," Quintares said, "I'll drop by sometime and take a look at your horses."

Feeling like a heel I dredged up a smile. "The latch-string's always out," I told him and took my departure.

It was a dirty trick I'd played on him and I felt like a Judas as I wound my way home. That it had been in a good cause made me feel no less guilty. The man was obviously a gentleman and I reckoned could be counted on to join no conspiracy against Terry's sheep.

I decided I'd better see Ace Jolly again. Perhaps I could defuse the powder train I'd laid. With Quintares having no hard feelings toward Terry's sheep, her future, while still dark, looked considerably brighter. If I could talk Mark out of mixing into this, I reckoned Barbona could hold his own against Jolly and any greasy sackers he could talk into joining him in whatever scheme he had in mind for getting rid of her sheep.

It was coming on toward dusk when I rode into the Tadpole yard for the second time that day and discovered Mark and Jolly with their heads together between house and barn. I had not expected to find Mark here, but perhaps it was just as well for him to hear what I had to say.

Mark Elder said when I pulled up a few feet away from them, "Ace figures Quintares is out to grab his range."

"Yes, but I told him this morning it was only a rumor. I've just come back from seeing Quintares and he's assured me there's no truth in it."

"What'd you expect him to say?" Ace snarled. "Hell, there's only three spreads it would pay him to jump, and neither yours nor the Circle Dot have a quarter of the water I've produced with my mills. It's *my* place he's after—I'll not believe any different!"

He folded thick arms across the breadth of his chest and gave me the look of a sore-footed bear. "By Gawd, I'll shoot the first Mex'kin puts his foot on my ground!"

I said to Mark, "I hope you're not swallowing that hogwash. Quintares hasn't hired even one new hand. He's no more intention—"

"It ain't your ground he's after," Ace yelled, and glared up at me with his bad teeth showing behind pulled-back lips.

"I dunno," Mark grunted. "Where there's smoke it's a pretty safe bet there's bound to be some fire. You can't trust these Mex'kins—look at Barbona! Throwin' in with Terry to get back at us cowmen!"

"Barbona," I said, "has good reason to hate cowmen. Anyway he's no Mexican, his mother was white as you are. If they'd left him alone up at Showlow he wouldn't be down here herdin' Terry's sheep."

"Never figured on you turnin' out to be a sheep lover. Messin' round with them horses you musta been out too long in that goddamn sun!" Ace sneered, looking ugly. "If you like sheep so much why don't you go over there an' join her?"

"Might be I will if you two start shootin'. Ace I can understand, but I thought better of you," I told Mark flatly. "How can you call yourself her friend? Scheming to—"

"Shut your face!" Mark's look was like two splinters of glass. "This is between me an' her. What I do ain't none of your put in! It was my ol' man set you up in the horse business an' you'll toe the line or I'll snatch you out of it— you got that clear?"

Those words snapped at me like the crack of a fist, opened up some thoughts I hadn't scrutinized before, and I stared at him, shaken, discovering in him now a man I hadn't known before.

In this brittle stillness, through the surge of my temper, I saw in shocked clarity some staggering truths. Caring no more for me than a piece of wastepaper, this man I'd thought a friend was the power-mad dog I'd painted Quintares to be in my talks with Ace Jolly. A man who'd strip Terrance of her possessions, thinking to leave her no alternative to marriage—prepared to crush anybody who got in his way. A man who'd seen in the sheep-hating Jolly a tool ready to his purpose.

CHAPTER
7

Riding home the whole complexion of what I'd glimpsed ahead of us had changed and not, I thought, for the better. It must have been Mark who'd turned Ace into this frightened and fanatical hater of sheep, carefully grooming him to spearhead the violence and be a believable scapegoat should current plans miscarry. It seemed plain enough now how little he actually cared for Terry; it was some hidden dream the man was in love with, the girl herself but a necessary cog in the wheel of his intentions.

Already top dog in the power structure here, could he have been seeking even greater influence? And what was it she had that made him so determined to marry her that, to his way of thinking, he would leave her no alternative and—under threat of foreclosure—force me to go along with him?

I just couldn't figure it. Every notion I latched on to appeared too farfetched, too loco for belief. But there had to be something back of it, bound to be plain enough once you caught on to it.

He was not, however, as shrewd as he imagined. In regard to me at any rate. I could deal myself a new hand by abandoning my land and taking my horses elsewhere. I had no hankering to do this, but had even less intention of taking orders from him.

"Hey, Edwardo! Where the hell are you?" I called as I rode through the gate and into my yard. He popped his head out the front door. "You had any visitors while I've been gone?"

He came out with a shotgun, shaking his head.

"There's a heap of queer things in the wind these days," I said to him dourly. "Be a good idea to keep that gun handy." That seemed pretty good advice for myself as well, and I took a sharp look around in the moonlight. Range wars and feuds touched everyone around in one fashion or another, and certainly my own actions weren't above suspicion.

I put up my horse inside the barn, broke open a fresh bale, pitched some alfalfa into his feed rack and got him some water. Another thought struck me as I went into the house and into the kitchen, where the Navajo kid was warming up leftover beans and sowbelly. Once Mark got all the mileage out of Jolly that could be gotten, what was to stop him from gobbling up the Tadpole along with the windmills and tanks Ace thought more of than he did his own crew?

There wasn't much to hinder him from getting rid of Ace.

After that, I reckoned, he'd be coming after me. And these horses I had pinned my hopes on. Right now Quintares was too big for him to tackle, but once he'd slapped his brand on Terry and got rid of Ace and me, I allowed he'd likely find some way of acquiring the Villalobos.

Probably I was overreacting to what I'd thought to read from his face when he had chucked me that threat. I kept rolling it over in my head while we ate and damn well reckoned I had better take steps while I still had the chance.

• • •

The first step I took was to visit the Circle Dot bright and early the next morning.

I had no real plans, was just figuring to test the water. So when I ran across Bill Hazel puttering at the day pen, where the ranch horses lifted their heads to nicker at Surefoot, I didn't quite know what to make of it. When it came to horse sense and savvy he was easily the best of the three hands Terry'd kept on after the death of her father.

"Havin' a holiday, Bill?" I asked as I came up.

All he fetched in answer was a grimace. "Ain't much to do since she took on them Yaquis. Barbona give orders they'll tend to the sheep. All we've got t' do is set on some high spot an' keep our eyes peeled for trouble. One of us at a time kin take care of that."

He sounded pretty disgruntled. I said, "Who's on watch now?"

"Dude's havin' that pleasure."

"Where's Reb Lockhart?"

"Tryin' t' git up more water outa that spring back of the bunkhouse."

I nodded and went on up to the house to find Terry and try out a notion that had just come to mind. As my horse crossed the yard Terry stuck her head out the door and put a smile on her face when she saw who it was. "Get down," she called, "and give your saddle a rest."

She had a dress on this morning instead of a blouse and jeans and a look on her face that showed the stress she was under. I said, "Thought I'd come by and see how you're makin' out."

"Guess you could say I'm still in possession." Her green eyes searched my face. "How are things with you?"

"Well as could be expected, I reckon." We considered each other, her lips still holding a piece of their smile, a touch of curiosity in the cant of her stare. "What brings you here so early?"

"Wondered if I could borrow one of your hands for three or four days?"

"Sure. Which one you want?"

"Bill Hazel, if you can spare him."

"Since Barbona's been taking care of the sheep I've had my work cut out finding enough to keep them busy." She pushed the hair back off her forehead. "Someone been slicing a gap in your fence?"

"No, nothin' like that." I dredged up a chuckle. "Just reckoned I might make some changes is all. Mark popped the question yet?"

The rest of the smile fell away from her lips. "That's all he wants to talk about lately. Mighty persuasive the way he lines up the so-called advantages. Haven't heard any offers from your direction."

I managed a grin. "Ain't got much to offer stacked up against him."

Her eyes, with their changeable shades, poked at my face for the longest while, must, I thought, have observed the squirming back of my attempt to appear unreadable. "In a race it's not always the swiftest that wins. Perhaps I'm not looking for material advantages," she pointed out brusquely. "Could be other things I look for in a man."

The challenge I read in the blunt directness of that green-eyed stare made my heart jump around like them wormy beans the Mexicans bet on, but I kept this elation buried inside me. I wanted her, sure, but saying so—the way I saw it—would be about the worst thing I could do for her right now if I'd sized Mark up right. Just the same it cost me considerable effort to let that go past without remark and say to her in my everyday voice, "If you don't mind then I'll pick up Bill and we'll shove along."

It felt like her stare hung on to me all the way to the corral but I refused to let myself look back. "Throw your hull on a horse," I said to Hazel. "I've fixed it up to borrow you a spell."

Back at my place, still not sure which way I was going to jump, the only thing I could think of to do with Bill Hazel was to have him top off the half dozen green-broke three-year-olds Edwardo had brought up and corraled in the day pen.

I wasn't frightened of Mark on my own account, for to close me out and get me off this place he'd have to go through channels and that would take a few days even with his amount of clout. First off he'd have to get a judgment against me and have papers served. By that time I could be gone with my horses. What I *was* worried about was the thought of him getting the notion Terry might be leaning toward me, in which case I'd little doubt he'd talk Ace into full-scale harassment.

Edwardo hadn't been taken into my confidence but was a good deal brighter than you might think to look at him in his runover boots, patched shirt and undented ten-gallon hat. With an unreadable face he asked, "Why you get new man to ride your horses?"

"Old hand," I said, "been working for Terry. Got him on loan in case we have to get the horses out of here in a hurry."

When he looked the question, I said, "Mark Elder's got a mortgage on this spread and I'm six weeks behind on the payments. He could grab the whole works if it happens to suit him. Long as I can help it he won't glom on to these nags, which means in plain English we might have to move quick."

"We go reservation?"

"By golly," I said, "hadn't thought about that," and took a searching look at him.

"My cousin take care of them. Be safe on reservation."

"Well, danged if they wouldn't. I'll keep it in mind." I chucked him a grin. "How old are you, Edwardo?"

"I have eighteen years. In old days be warrior—count coup."

I nodded. "Might get a chance yet. You keep that scattergun handy."

My land, like I've said, is up in the hills, but not too far from the stretched-out flats where Jolly had his tanks and mills, where cows in his brand—and sometimes others— oftentimes came when they were hunting a drink. I was in the corral helping Bill Hazel top off those broncs when we heard the shots. There were only two, but as I pulled up to listen, Bill said, "Rifles. Somebody knockin' over a rabbit for the pot." And, when he saw my face, added, "Wouldn't be any of our bunch—too far away. Besides, she's give orders we're to stay out of trouble."

When we knocked off for the day and headed for the house those two shots were still banging through my head. I hoped to hell Bill was right about them.

CHAPTER
8

The following morning showed an overcast sky to match the mood I had gone to bed with; the only light spot kicking its heels in my view of the future came from the kid's remark about hiding my horses on the reservation. His cousin ran sheep and with the proper bribe might, I thought, be induced to stray them into these hills.

That kind of notion could be worth some hard thinking.

I sat on the porch steps to indulge my fancy with no faith in those clouds as a herald of rain; they'd been round before—or others just like them, with never a leak. But Navajo sheep coming through these hills might just possibly spike Mark's guns, laying him open to all manner of charges.

Reservation Navajos were wards of the government. Any rumpus involving them could bring federal marshals, and those weren't no boys to go stamping your boot at. They didn't care about clout and could reduce Mark's schemes to ashes right quick. Given provocation.

While I was basking in this cheerful thought and Bill Hazel was back in the round pen working with the broncs, who should come riding into my yard but this same spurious friend I'd been thinking about.

Like the cock of the walk he imagined himself to be, Mark pulled up fronting the porch to look me over. "Ain't you gettin' a mite too large for your britches hirin' top hands to do your work? Settin' there like a toad under a cabbage leaf payin' owed money for what a growed man could do for himself."

"Not feelin' too chipper this mornin'," I said.

"Well, that's too damn bad," he remarked in a sneering bullypuss tone. "My ol' man was a sucker for sentiment—easiest touch in the Four Corners country. But it's me you got to deal with now. I'll give you some advice, an' till you pay back what's owin', Gill, you better step careful. Now you send that feller right back where he come from and you stay plumb away from the Circle Dot—you got that?"

When I kept my mouth shut a nasty grin spread across that hard mouth. "I'm not a man what gives a rapp for dependents. You better get that straight. There's just two kinds of people camped on this range, them that's for me an' them that ain't. I don't want to get harsh with a boy I've known most of my life, but I can have you out of here any time it suits me. That's a fact you can frame an' hang above your bed."

It was plain he liked to hear himself talk. He had the family resemblance, but now with all pretense cast aside it was all I could find in common with his father. Making ready to leave he dropped a final warning.

"Stay out of my way an' you've got nothin' to worry you. Try crossin' me up," he said with that sharp ugly look peering out of his stare, "an' I'll flatten you like last year's leaf!"

Sitting there seething I watched him take the trail to the Circle Dot.

Coming out of the corral after finishing his stint, Bill Hazel asked with his eyes on mine, "What was that all about?"

"Guess he figured I might be in need of a little guidance." I said through stiff lips, "Told me to send you back where you came from."

"You gonna do it?"

"No."

"What'll he do?"

"Expect he'll take the place away from me when he gets around to it. Old D.J. set me up with this deal. Ranch holds a mortgage. I'm six weeks behind on the current payment."

"A fine kettle of fish."

"Yeah, well . . . that's the way it goes."

"No way of payin' it?"

I shrugged. "None that I can locate. I got enough to pay half and that's about it."

"What about these bangtails?" he said with a meaningful look. "How many are there?"

"About forty right now."

"He goin' to grab them, too?"

"Not if I can help it," I said. "Soon's he notifies the sheriff I figure to get them out of here—put 'em beyond his reach if I can."

"Might take a bit of doin'," he said and scowled.

"You're not obliged to help," I said. "Only fair to say there might be some risk in it," I mentioned, eyeing him. "Aims to squash anyone gets in his way."

Bill Hazel snorted. "Where you aimin' to take 'em?"

"I did think maybe I could cut a deal with Quintares."

"Think he'd go for it?"

"I believe he would. But Edwardo has suggested driving them onto the reservation. He's got a sheep-raisin' cousin over there he thinks would take 'em." I said, "Have to move them at night of course. Even so it could be touch an' go—damn good chance to get a harp an' a halo."

Hazel snorted again. "Count me in. What the hell are friends for?"

CHAPTER
9

Sky didn't look no better after we'd eaten a noon meal of skillet-fried beans and I was back on the porch trying to yank some sense from the jumble of thoughts prowling round through my head. It was a gun-metal color, pretty much like my thinking. I hadn't yet reached the beleaguered plight of the Circle Dot but was sure as hell headed that way in a hurry.

I couldn't see that my undercover moves had much helped anyone unless it was Mark; might as well say I'd helped push Ace Jolly in the very direction Mark wanted him to go. But it was plain Mark knew where my sympathies lay and I reckoned he figured he had spiked my guns. I could still join Terry openly in her attempt to survive, except what kind of fool would risk his neck in a cause I had to feel was already lost?

A fellow might perhaps shove a wrench in Mark's schemes by throwing more sheep on the public lands from a different quarter—if he had the sheep and didn't care what happened to them. It would force the man to embroil himself openly, drag him out from behind the cover of his stalking horse, Jolly. Before he was ready to have folks know what he was up to. But the more I turned this notion over the less faith I had in it.

If he'd sufficient confidence to threaten me as he had, he was probably far enough along in his purpose to barrel right on with it regardless. Countering his intentions by bringing in more sheep would almost certainly not stop him, merely make them more expensive and create a bigger racket.

No club I could lay hand to looked to have sufficient weight.

I very probably couldn't talk Edwardo's reservation cousin into invading public lands, his risks would be too great; no Navajo could be that stupid. On the whole they were a pretty smart people. They weren't any longer compelled to stay on the reservation, but to take their sheep onto public lands would undoubtedly anger the Great White Father and bring dire retribution.

All my cogitations looked to be helping Terry not a bit, nor myself.

The afternoon was half gone when distant motion caught my attention, and I discovered a horsebacker approaching and got off my rump to watch him come through the gate, politely closing it after him.

First thing that grabbed me as he rode into the yard was the horse he was forking. It was one of my own, the horse I had sold that gambler who had been in such a hurry to get out of the country.

This newcomer wasn't garbed as that one had been, but the same hard look had been ground into him. He was clad in dust-covered jeans and a shield-fronted shirt of dark flannel with a long-used hat tugged low above sharp eyes, one side of the floppy brim pinned against the crown with a cactus thorn. "I see," he said with a snaggletoothed grin, "you recognize the horse."

"It's one I sold a couple weeks back."

"Yes," he said and nodded, biting off a fresh chew, "one I collected as part payment on a debt. Understand there's trouble bein' brewed around here; thought mebbe you could use a little help."

He had pulled up his mount a few feet from the porch, near enough for me to catch a whiff of sheep. "Aren't you takin' a lot for granted?"

"I don't think so." He grinned, flicking an eye over at Hazel, who was drifting up from the corral. "I been through this neighborhood a time or two before, sort of gettin' the feel of things. You got a woman here tryin' to raise sheep in cattle country, which is enough right there to fetch the smell of trouble." He spat and grinned some more. Hooking a leg round the horn he said, "On top of that you got an ambitious cowman figurin' to bend this situation to where he kin add a spread or two to what he's already got."

He settled complacently back with that knowing look and observed when he got no argument, "Added to which he holds a mortgage on this piece of ground and reckons to tie your hands with it. From where I sit you both need help and you're lookin' at a man who'll be happy to extend it."

"Why?"

"Sheer brotherly love—why else would I be stickin' my neck out?"

"Why else indeed?" Bill Hazel said scornfully.

"Would you believe that sonuvabitch owes me somethin'?"

"Sounds a mite pat," I said with a rummaging glance. "You don't look the sort to succor the needy without there's something in it for Number One."

"Well, I'm not," he declared, beaming on me like a teacher discovering an unexpectedly bright student. "You got the right of it there." He spat a stream of juice at a pumping lizard that turned it brown as a curl of old leather.

"I've got a gather of hungry sheep back a piece that would like mighty well to get onto them flats. I believe in the Good Book—smite the Philistines hip an' thigh."

I got to admit this fellow intrigued me. Flamboyant he might well be, but if he had the sheep he came handy to our need, no getting around that. Naturally I had a few reservations but told him gruffly, "Get down an' set a spell. Might as well talk it over." As we took chairs on the porch I grumbled, "Whereabouts are you from if that's not askin' too much?"

"Name's Tolliver," he mentioned, "Joe Tolliver. No need to go into my antecedents. I got the sheep an' kin sure as hell put 'em right where they're needed."

"Be buckin' a pat hand you put your nose in here."

"Got a cure for pat hands," he said with a grin, slapping the holstered gun at his hip. "I don't figger to lose over fifty sheep, an' I'd give that many to put 'em on Bar B Cross grass. Told D.J. I'd be back one day an' here I am, plumb rarin' t' go."

"Ain't D.J. you'll be buckin'," I said. "It's his son's in charge now."

Bill Hazel spoke up to say, "Different breed of cat—"

"All cats look alike t' me, young feller."

"I been tryin'," I said, "to avoid spillin' blood."

"You ain't gonna do it," he came back at me flatly. "I been through this kinda ruckus before. Only way you kin stop a bullheaded cow baron who figgers he sets at the right hand of God—blood an' plenty of it!"

CHAPTER
10

"If we come to any understandin'," I said, "you're goin' to have to hold back till I give the word." I told him how I had this thing figured; wound up by saying, "I don't want that girl hurt."

"Course you don't," Tolliver replied, "an' if this cow waddy's aim is t' marry her, she won't be. What he's up to, accordin' to your tell, is t' back her into a corner where the only choice she'll have is t' marry him or lose not only her sheep but the ranch t' boot. But what you've done is slip a wild card into this deal—Barbona. I've knowed Piki for years. He'll do whatever looks good to him. There ain't one reasonable bone in his head."

I had enough on my plate without listening to that. "Never mind," I said, "I'll take care of Piki. How many sheep are you aimin' to risk and where are they?"

"Six hundred head in three different bands. They're in a gov'ment reserve an' nobody'll see 'em till I'm ready to move. I'll have 'em on the ground inside twenty-four hours from the time you give the word," he said, getting up. "Meantime I'll send you one of my men. When you're ready for me to hit Elder you put him up on one of them

53

fast horses. We'll go through Bar B Cross like Sherman through Atlanta."

After Tolliver had ridden off into the dusk I said to Bill Hazel, "What do you think?"

"I think," Hazel said, dragging a hand across his bristled jaw, "he's plumb right about Barbona. He's a take-over hombre an' havin' him around is like jugglin' thawed dynamite!"

"I know," I said, scowling, "but at the time I got him there was no one else to call on who'd even make a pretense at keepin' that cow bunch away from Terry's sheep. I didn't like it and I don't much like lettin' this jasper in, but if I've pegged Mark right we've got damn little choice. There's times when you have to fight fire with fire or say good-bye to everything you hold dear. What I was askin' is what you think of Tolliver."

"Man with a grudge and one that ain't come into this blind."

"That's the way I've got him down. That horse he's on I sold a couple weeks back to a poker-faced galoot who was in a real sweat to get out of this region. Seems he was tryin' to get away from Tolliver."

"Which shows Tolliver," Hazel added, "to be a man that collects his debts. Wonder what he had against old D.J.?"

"Whatever it is I'd say Mark's inherited it along with that ranch. What I wonder is how much like Barbona he's going to turn out to be. I'm like a man's got a bear by the tail with each hand."

Edwardo put in a full night of snoring, much the same as usual. I didn't sleep a lot and probably Hazel didn't either. My thoughts kept going round like a horse on a treadmill, and the little I slept relieved neither me nor my problems any noticeable amount.

During a breakfast of refried beans washed down with coffee thick enough to float, I was rummaging through the dregs of my thinking and Hazel wanted to know how I summed up Terry's plight.

"Uncomfortable," I said, "an' like to get worse."

"You still figurin' to move these caballos?"

"Expect I'll have to."

"You must hate like sin leavin' all this fence."

"Old D.J. hung that fence around my neck; if I was going in for high-priced horses, he said, I had to have fence. It's that goddamn wire that's run up the cost an' the prime reason why I'm behind in my payments."

"You still goin' to take 'em onto the reservation?"

"If they have to be moved."

"Villalobos would be closer, easier to get to."

I looked at him carefully. "Spit it out. What is it about going up there you don't like?"

"Well, it ain't exactly that. What if this cousin of Edwardo's ain't prepared to take 'em?"

"He take 'em," Edwardo said, bobbing his head. "He like fast horse."

"I'll bet," Bill Hazel growled, eyeing me significantly. "What I been thinkin' is . . . could be a heap easier to get 'em there than get 'em back, if you get what I mean."

Edwardo's face hadn't changed but I could see this turn in the talk didn't please him. "Wish I knew," I said, "how far away from here those sheep are."

"Thought Tolliver said they were in the Forest Reserve?"

"What he said was government reserve—could be they're in that new Park Reserve Teddy's just set aside for the folks that come after us. Which is a damn sight closer."

"You think he figures to cross us up?"

"Guess we'll just have to wait and see."

Scarcely four hours later Tolliver's man showed up all grins and politeness. He was a squatty looking man with a dark cast of countenance hinting at Yaqui blood in his veins, pants held up by a twist of rope, cast in one eye and two fingers gone from the middle of one hand. He caught me eyeing this. "Rurales done that," he grunted. "Come within an inch of gittin' my hair." He whipped off his battered black hat to exhibit the scar across his left temple. Said with nice irony we could call him Mexico.

Made himself right at home after putting his horse up and forking him some of my expensive alfalfa. Very competent fellow with enough assurance to find his way into the best chair on the porch. "When you boys fixin' to eat?" he inquired.

Hazel said, "Around here we eat after dark. When there's nothin' else to do."

The fellow let that sail right over his head. Thinking Hazel looked minded to cuff him, I sent Bill off to work some more of the broncs Edwardo had fetched in off the back four hundred. I asked the man how long he'd been in this country, having noticed he seemed pretty handy with the lingo.

"Oh"—he grinned—"I been here a good while off an' on."

"How long you been with Tolliver?" I asked.

"Since," he said, "I was about so high," and set a hand about two feet off the planks. "What else would you like to know?"

I narrowed my eyes at him. "You one of his herders?"

"More like errand boy. Reckon that's what you'd call it." He returned my stare blandly, no whit taken aback by my look.

"I might have to move out of here quick. How many sheep has he got out there?"

"Reckon you'd have to ask him that."

"Take a guess," I said. "More than six hundred?"

"I'm not very much at his camps these days."

"Wouldn't think in that case you'd be much good at your job."

"Oh, I'm usually around when he's errands to be run."

I took a fresh grip on my temper and was turning away when Ace Jolly rode into the yard with three of his crew, an unprecedented occurrence. In a foul mood to start with I expect I stared pretty rude at this intrusion, but I said coolly enough, "Looks like you boys are loaded for bear."

Jolly peered at the porch. "Who's that lookin' like he just bought the place?"

"Fellow hunting a job."

"From what Elder says I don't see how you can afford to be hirin'. No point to it anyway. Mark's figgerin' t' make a line camp of this place. Tells me you're only here on sufferance. You git rid of that Circle Dot hand like he told you?"

Very conscious of the poor figure I cut in the light of Jolly's disparaging words, wondering too if he'd got orders to move me, I said, perhaps a bit reckless, "Until the sheriff serves papers on me you can tell your friend Elder I'll be stayin' right here."

"That's pretty bold talk from a fancy-ass squatter!" he remarked, looking ugly.

"You want to find out how bold I can get stick around another minute and you're like to find out."

Ace turned his horse to move back through the gate they'd left open, the others turning with him, Jolly pausing long enough to snarl back across their shoulders. "If we wasn't in a hustle to git t' the Circle Dot—"

I said, "If that's where you're headin' you better find another way. That trail's no longer open."

"Since when?"

"Since right now. You want to see some empty saddles just try goin' up there."

"You can't—"

"Try me," I said quietly, and half the belligerence fell out of his stare. Wheeling his horse he sent it streaking toward the flats, his three hands spurring after him.

I didn't look at Tolliver's errand boy, but if the fellow hadn't been sitting there taking all this in I might not have been so goddamn brash. I strode off toward the barn knowing I'd put my foot in it proper. That sonofabitch was going straight back to Mark.

CHAPTER
11

The clouds still hovered. In this sticky heat I prowled around, edgy, looking for things that might need doing, and finally gave up and went into the barn, which was where Hazel found me.

He said nothing about the snout of that rifle I'd glimpsed peering up at those fellows from just inside the door. I didn't either, but couldn't help wondering if Ace had seen it and if this wasn't why he'd taken off in such a fury. I said, "If Barbona takes it into his head to start things hittin' the skids, contrary to what I told him, you might be needed back there and I'd need to know."

I had already sent Edwardo off through the hills to put Terry on guard, and in this jittery mood that had sunk its claws into me it was in my mind we probably both of us should go except that . . .

"What did you tell him?"

"Told him not to start anything, that if there had to be killing to let those cowprodders drop the first man."

"All he'd have to do to make sure of that," Hazel grumbled, "is to push Terry's sheep out onto them flats."

I said gloomily, "I suppose so."

"If that damn Ace went scamperin' back to Mark you can look for the sheriff to be showin' up most any time. We ought to rustle up the rest of your horses and get the hell out of here."

The thought of Mark walking through my house was chewing on me like an ulcerated tooth, and my imminent departure had my eyes roving round like I was about to say good-bye to some dear one whose absence would leave a powerful hole in my life.

Hazel, eyeing me, said, "I had a little place somethin' like this once—took me the best part of a year to git over it. But you ain't lost it yet. If we get out of here straightaway there'll be no one to serve the papers on and it'll still be yours until they can catch up with you."

I could see that of course, but the notion of Mark's hands taking over and turning the place into a hog waller damn near changed my mind about leaving.

"Don't be a chump!" Hazel growled at me sharply. "With them horses to gather we better be movin'."

It was crowding two hours before we got back with the rest of my horses and pulled up in the dooryard for a last look around. While Hazel was fetching the ones I'd kept in the barn and letting the broncs we'd been gentling out of the corral, I got Mexico up on the slowest fast horse I could think of.

"What's up?" he said, swiveling his look from me to Hazel and back again. "Looks like you're fixin' to light a shuck outa here."

"That's the general idea. Fling your gear on this horse an' cut a bee line for Tolliver. We're not waitin' for the Bar B Cross to latch on to these bangtails."

He had his good eye fixed on me with suspicion. "Why all the rush?"

"I'm not minded," I said, "to lose these horses. By this

time Jolly will have got to Mark Elder. Elder holds my note and will be sending for the sheriff—"

"Once we hit the flats with those sheep," Tolliver's errand boy scoffed, "them cow wallopers'll be havin' no time to be thinkin' about sheriffs!"

I said, "That's as may be. I'm taking no chances on this deal foulin' up."

"Tolliver don't foul up, you kin take it from me."

"You're welcome to stick around if you want. We're gettin' out of here. Pronto," I said. "I told your boss I'd put you on a fast horse. You're on one—do as you like." We left on the run.

We let them run long enough to shake the high spirits out of them and then as dusk settled over us dropped them into a slogging walk. By the cavalry system of walk and trot a fairly decent horse could make five to six miles an hour and, if things went right, by morning we would be halfway to the reservation and, hopefully, a safe haven.

"I take it you plan to come back," Hazel said.

"I sure ain't fixing to run out on Terry if that's what you're thinking."

"Never reckoned you were."

"Seems likely," I predicted, "if Tolliver's outfit can keep Mark tied up, Barbona's Yaquis ought to be able to handle Jolly."

"Providin' Mark hasn't sent half his crew with Ace, which he prob'ly has."

I hadn't reckoned on that, but thinking about it I was inclined to agree. Mark, from what I'd seen of him lately, would be aiming to make quick work of this business and grab all the range he could straightaway. Terry's sheep to my revised notions had become just an excuse. A means, he figured, of maneuvering her into marriage.

It was hard for me to believe he could be such a bastard but there had been, as I looked back, a number of indications I'd passed off as bravado. He wasn't fooling; he meant to grab all the range he could shove his cows onto. He had already shown he didn't give two hoots for what folks might think of him.

Keeping these horses together with the night grown black as the ace of spades put a strain on our attention. That first wild run had worked most of the spookiness out of them, but in any band of horses there will always be a few bunch-quitters wanting to strike out on their own. Some cows have the same inclination.

It was gruelling work but I judged we were making pretty fair time. We were beyond the hills now, on the far side of the Four Corners range, and by a deal of hard riding pointing them straight at the reservation. A lopsided moon had come out of the east and this helped some to keep the stretched-out line on track.

On this easier terrain I got to wondering what I would do if Edwardo's uncle refused to take them under his wing, or those who managed their affairs—like maybe the Agent— refused to let him.

It was near three o'clock when Edwardo rejoined us. I asked about Terry, and he said he'd alerted her to the possibility of a visit from Jolly, that at the time he had left her there had been no untoward incidents.

"And Barbona?" I asked.

"He was with the sheep, him and the Yaquis."

I sent him on up ahead, for he was a lot more familiar with this region than I was and might save us a few miles. After a while Hazel dropped back to join me while the horses were walking.

"Have you figured out," Hazel asked, "what you will do if they turn us away?"

"With things like they are we can't afford to be tied down. If we can't leave them there I guess we'll have to try Quintares."

"And if he won't take them?"

I shook my head. "In that event we'll be in a real bind. Now that Mark's dug up the hatchet and about to go on the warpath we're going to have to get back to the Circle Dot, no two ways about that."

We stepped up the pace and rode for half an hour without further talk, but when we dropped back into that ground-covering walk I said out of my thinking, "Aside from natural inclination and the fact that Terry's about the finest hunk of woman in the Four Corners country, can you think of any compelling reason why Mark is so damn hell-bent to marry her?"

"Only reason I can come up with is he's doin' it to spite you. Way I see it he's always resented you, and now that his old man's out of the way he figures to cut you right out of the picture."

I thought about it some more without turning up any better notion. It would hurt like hell to see her shackled to him, but no matter how much he might have secretly hated me all this while, even combined with his intention of throwing me off my place, I couldn't be satisfied I had the whole story.

When the first pink streaks crept above the distant hills we stopped for an hour's rest, eating jerky out of our saddlebags while the horses browsed on the brittle stalks of burnt dry grass.

CHAPTER
12

The big trouble with me in this whole frightening business was lack of experience. Like a kid who has found himself in a quagmire, I'd no way of knowing what to trust or where to turn. I was lost in a maze of changed relationships, stumbling through perils I had never encountered. With eyes abruptly opened to the real world about me, I had to cross shaky ground by the miserable process of thrusting one foot ahead of the other, expecting any moment each step could be the last.

When we pushed on again the last vestige of pink had gone out of the east; the leaden overcast stretched in all directions, grimly gray and without so much as a single crack, as rough on the outlook as a circling of buzzards. Only when our outfit hit up a lope was I briefly jolted loose of dark imaginings, my eyes too busy to dwell on inner turmoil.

It was just past noon when I spied the first smoke. Against the murk of that vast stretch of clouds I couldn't be sure of what I was looking at and thought at first it was probably a dust devil. But then I discovered another halfway across the view ahead and to the left, this one a single straight-up smudge above the dark line of hills.

Twisting in the saddle for a quick look behind I found another smudge there—this undeniably dust. Swiveling round I found Bill Hazel's gaze locked in the same direction.

Edwardo came pelting back to swing his mount alongside Surefoot. "San Carlos Apaches!"

"How do you know?" I rasped at him, jolted.

"In here I know," he cried, thumping his chest, the other hand pushing black hair from his face. "No Navajos there—renegade Apaches ride under that dust!"

Probably took one Indian to recognize another. "Come on," I growled, "let's get these hides movin'."

With our horses pushed into a run once more I tried to calculate our chances. The Apaches' ponies were almost bound to be fresher but of nondescript breeding. With any luck, I thought, my own bred for speed should be able to keep ahead of them. And should have enough bottom even yet to do it.

When, later, I turned for another look the pursuing dust seemed farther behind, but still there, still coming. They weren't likely to give up without they lost us completely which, considering the amount of ground we had already covered, didn't seem probable.

If as Edwardo claimed these were Apaches, I could see no good in prodding the kid to get us out of this; his neck was as much at risk as ours, and if he knew of any way of eluding them I reckoned he would take it. I sent him on up ahead to ride point again, allowing our hard-pushed horses to fall back into a walk once more.

There were no warmongering tribes in this region nor, despite some grumbling, much likelihood of an outbreak; but with any group of Indians chafing under imposed restraints there were always a few young bucks eager to get into any deviltry that offered and horses like ours were greatly prized.

After half an hour of slogging along at a walk it became apparent our pursuers were beginning to edge nearer. I still couldn't see anything but their dust, but I was in such a turmoil as to wonder apprehensively if it wouldn't perhaps be better, if we could find a motte of trees, to pull up and wait for them, to fight it out and be done with this.

The same thought evidently had been romping through Hazel's head. With a lifted hand he came dashing over. "According to Edwardo there's a good-sized depression up ahead about a mile. Maybe we oughta duck into it and pick off a few of them!"

"If we can stay ahead of them," I yelled back at him, "I'd rather keep goin'."

So we skirted the depression and sent our bangtails into throwing up dust again swiftly pushing them into a gallop. Twenty minutes of this showed the redskins dropping behind once more but staying doggedly after us. It seemed to me our fate would be decided by endurance, and while I was sure our horses were faster, those Indian ponies in addition to being agile were surprisingly tough. I was not at all certain we'd be able to outlast them.

As the chase wore into the shank of the afternoon, even going all out it grew plain our bunch had lost most of that extra zip I'd been counting on. But when I looked back I couldn't find even the dust of our pursuers. Had we lost them or did someone among them know more about this terrain than Edwardo?

A damn sticky question with another batch of hills less than a couple miles ahead, these being bound to slow us down even more. We allowed our tired hides to drop into a walk and I pushed old Surefoot ahead for a talk with Hazel.

I said, "What do you think? You reckon we've lost them?"

Terry's hand said, "I don't reckon so. More like they've probably called it a day. We're not more'n three or four miles from our goal—we're already on the reservation. When we git up higher you'll see the Agent's house."

I don't mind admitting I took the first comfortable breath I'd drawn since those buggers had taken after us. And half an hour later I could see the Agent's clapboard house where it sat like a mother hen in a clutter of corrals and one-room adobes.

By the time old Surefoot brought me up to the Agent's quarters I could see Edwardo standing outside the gate of his picket fence, haranguing a long stringbean of a man in a snap-brim hat and the kind of clothes I understand they wear in Boston. "That's the Agent," Hazel said, pulling up beside me. "Jeremiah Galpin."

"He's not goin' to let us in," Edwardo called.

CHAPTER
13

Bill Hazel and I swapped alarmed glances.

"Did you say we had planned to leave them with your kinfolks?"

"He says feed's short and won't stretch to outside horses."

Hazel swore. "Did you tell him," I said, "we been chased near all day by a bunch of hostiles?"

"I told him."

"Keep these critters bunched," I growled and neck-reined Surefoot over to the fence. "Do you realize," I asked the Agent, "that if you refuse to allow these horses to remain here you'll be driving them and us straight into the guns of those hostiles?"

He stared up at me imperturbably. "There are no hostiles in this vicinity."

"Well, damn it," I said, getting hot under the collar, "they been after us all day!"

"You're mistaken," he assured me. "We have no hostile Indians in Arizona."

"How long have you been in charge here, Galpin?"

"No use trying to upset my temper. I know my duty to

the government's wards. I'll not bandy words with you. If you don't remove those horses from this reservation at once I'll have the Indian police here do it for you."

"You stupid son of a bitch," I said, "if one of us manages ever to see town again an account of your action is going straight to Washin'ton!"

The Agent scraped up a frosty smile. "If that is supposed to reverse my decision you are wasting your breath. I've been threatened before," he declared with a contemptuous look and, raising his voice, called, "Shonto! Vya! I want these beasts driven off the reservation immediately. See to it."

Eyeing the two Indians coming up on the run I was minded to reach over that fence and take hold of him. The foremost Navajo blew a blast on his whistle and redskins came hurrying from every direction.

Surrounded by overwhelming numbers we left.

With our shadows bouncing long across hills directly east of us we took our tired horses down onto the tawny sands of the desert as that brief flash of sun fell behind the distant peaks. The only glimmer of hope I could find in our ejection came from knowing full dark was but short minutes away.

Under cover of night there was just a bare chance we might elude those Apaches if, contrary to Hazel's notion, they had not yet given up. I was pretty sure in my own mind they were still out there somewhere, reluctant to believe they might not have another whack at us. Horses such as these didn't come their way very often.

They couldn't know, I thought, we'd been bound for the reservation. Following their usual custom in situations such as this they'd probably split up into twos and threes to prowl the wastes till they came on to us again. It was generally credited by whiteskins that Indians disliked fighting at

night, but I put no stock in these old wives' tales. To grab
this kind of booty they'd dare a great deal in my opinion
and I reckoned we'd better stay doubly alert.

"I don't think we'll run into them," Hazel opined, "though
I'll freely confess I've no more desire to part with my hair
than you have. Seems to me, if they *are* still out there,
they'll figure we're bound to head south where we could
expect to find help."

"Yes," I said, "so we'll strike north for a spell, then east
a ways before taking off for the Villalobos."

We kept our charges to a shuffling walk, both to keep
down the noise and because our vision with no moon or
stars was greatly reduced. This made for slow going, and
with nerves stretched taut no one cared to make unnecessary
conversation.

After about an hour of uninterrupted progress we swung
to the east, hoping we had got around any possible search-
ers: I wasn't too confident we had, but our horses were in no
shape to risk avoidable miles. If you've never been in this
sort of situation you've no idea of the thoughts conjured,
the phantoms created by overwrought minds. Each bush,
each patch of deeper black, became a crouching redskin.
The fact that none of these imagined demons leapt upon
us with or without bloodcurdling cries did little to put our
fears at rest.

We must have been at least four hours from the reservation when finally I decided to go for broke and turned our
outfit in what I believed to be the direction of Quintares'
hacienda.

Still at a walk we slogged along through the murk of
diminished vision for another couple hours before pulling
up to give the horses a breather. Near as I could figure we
were about thirty miles from Quintares' range and perhaps
twenty-five from the Circle Dot. We'd got out of our sad-

dles to stretch the cramps from our legs and were having a muttered consultation when Edwardo abruptly grabbed on to my arm. "Shh!"

Through the stillness of the night, in the far off dark, we heard the oncoming rumor of hard-running hoofs. I don't know what thoughts this wild tearing through the dark put into the heads of my companions as I stood rigidly staring, hands clutching my rifle, but I could not believe this racket came from Apaches. It seemed to be coming from off toward the hills in the direction of the Circle Dot. Or perhaps from my own place.

Edwardo, when I'd sent him over there, would obviously have told Terry I had had it in mind to hide my horses on the reservation, and this appeared to be where the sounds were headed. "Stay here," I said, and flung myself in the saddle, kneeing Surefoot on a course that should intercept them.

It was risky, yes, but I had to find out.

They were moving so fast I had to put Surefoot into a run, and even so I barely got there in time. There were three of them, riding low-crouched above the necks of their horses. I let out a yell thinking to recognize Terry. It caught them in mid-stride and took near seventy feet to get their animals slowed enough to wheel them round and let me come up to them. Terry's voice called, "Is that you, Gracious?" like she couldn't quite believe it.

CHAPTER
14

In the gray of false dawn I made out her two hands, Lockhart and Inman, sitting their heaving horses behind her. "Yeah," I said, "what's up? You all right?"

"I guess I'm the only one who is!"

Which was when, peering over her shoulder, I spotted Inman's bandaged head, discovered the bloody rag round Lockhart's hand and stared at her, startled.

She said in a shaking voice, "We were trying to find you—"

"What's happened?"

"Jolly's crew with four of Mark's hands hit our sheep near the drop-off. While the Yaquis were trying to drive them away, Mark with his other three hands slipped in off that trail that goes past your place and surprised Reb and Dude, ordered them to drop their guns, and when Dude didn't move quick enough one of those devils shot him— but that's not the worst. The man's a maniac!" she cried, all a-tremble.

"You talking about Mark?"

"I certainly am! There has to be something wrong with him . . . I don't know why we didn't see it before. It was late yesterday afternoon, almost dark, when he called me out of the house. Two of his men were dragging Reb toward the woodpile. He said . . . he said if I didn't agree to marry him at once Reb was due to be made an example of. I said, 'You're crazy!'

"He looked it, too—I thought he was going to strike me. Instead he told them to get Reb over to the chopping block. Reb was struggling but couldn't get loose, and Mark's other hand had a gun dug into Duke's ribs. They kicked Reb's legs out from under him, dragged him over to the block and clamped an arm down on it. Mark grabbed up the axe and yelled at me, 'Unless you agree right now to marry me I'm going to take something off him.' "

She was shaking again, calling up the scene in her head it looked like. "I couldn't believe he would do such a thing. They had Reb's hand spread out on that block . . . Mark . . . Mark . . ." She couldn't go on.

Then she pulled up her head, cried in an agonized, half-hysterical voice, "They hauled me back into the house . . . where my mother was. They . . . they stood her up against the wall. 'Last chance,' he shouted. 'You going to do it or ain't you?' "

The tears were streaming down her face, she was shaking all over in the remembrance of horror.

I said aghast, "You're sayin' he shot her?"

She couldn't speak. Dude Inman said, "He sure did! I think the feller's gone clean off his rocker—"

"What happened then?"

Reb Lockhart said, "That old cook they've got rode into the yard, wild eyed an' hollering like a stuck pig that the Bar B Cross was filled with sheep, and Mark an' his hellions went tearin' off. Dude an' me ran into the house. Terry was on the floor unconscious and the old lady was dead."

"We better tend to that hand."

Reb growled, "Never mind that, all he done was smash my fingers."

"Lucky it was your left."

"Yeah," he said grimly.

And Dude said, "He's left-handed."

I searched Lockhart's face. "Can you use it at all?"

"I got another one, ain't I?" He said it like it was unfinished business.

The man had guts. Dude Inman said, "C'mon, let's git outa here."

"Wait," I said. "We've got the horses here. I think we better get back to the Circle Dot."

I led them back to where Hazel and Edwardo, knees crooked round their horns, sat waiting. When I'd given them the gist of what I'd been told Hazel said, "What about these horses?"

"Reckon we'll have to take them with us. We've got to find out what's happened back there—about the sheep, I mean, and Barbona's Yaquis."

It was around ten o'clock, with the sun intermittently peering through the clouds, when we reached the Circle Dot and penned up my horses in two of the corrals. Terry, looking far from her usual self but composed, told Hazel to see that they were fed and not to let them have too much water. Edwardo dug the grave while I hammered together a makeshift casket and we buried Mrs. O'Brian on a little knoll behind the house in solemn ceremony. I had fully expected Terry to break down, but she stood dry-eyed with a hand gripping mine. Then I sent Edwardo to find out about the sheep.

As best she could Terry had washed and rebandaged Reb Lockhart's smashed hand and changed the dressing on Inman's head, which he stoutly maintained was nothing but a gouge. "Just bounced off my skull," he said with a lopsided grin. "Nothin' to make all this fuss about."

After that I put my hull back on Surefoot and rode off to see what I could learn about the sheep. Before I'd covered more than a mile Barbona and his Yaquis came up out of a wash on the horses I'd sold him. "Left your Navajo tendin' the woollies," Piki said, coming straight to the point. "Like you told me, I let them bastards have the first shot. They nailed one of my men and we dropped two of theirs, but half the sheep got run over that cliff. Our best wasn't good enough to save the whole lot. We did nick a couple or mebbe three more of 'em before they pulled out, but that's it."

I told him what had happened at the house. "I'll get on back and try and figure what we better do next."

Barbona said, "I'll leave my boys with Edwardo but I'll set in with you on this figgerin'."

There wasn't, it seemed like, a heap that we could do aside from trying to protect what was left of Terry's sheep and making sure the Circle Dot wasn't invaded again by someone trying to slip in the back way. "I think Mark will be too busy for a while to cook up anything else," I said, and told Barbona about the six hundred sheep Tolliver's boys had shoved onto the Bar B Cross while Mark was off raising hell up here.

Barbona said, "I know that Tolliver. Tough as they come. He'll stay on that grass till there ain't a blade left."

It was finally decided that Barbona would rejoin the four Yaquis he had left, and the rest of us—Terry, her three ranch hands and myself—would stay at the house, take care of the horses and make sure anyone coming up past my place would get a hot lead welcome. I concluded the conference by reminding all and sundry that the cow crowd would shed no tears over any of us.

"What about those folks away out on the fringe of things, the ones Mark calls squatters?" Terry asked, trying, I thought, to haul herself from that black mood of despair.

"What about them?" I asked, to help her along with it.

"Well, there must be at least a dozen of them. Couldn't we get them to throw in with us?"

Hazel said, "Once Mark gets those sheep off his place it's a pretty sure bet he'll go after them, too. As for helping us, forget it. That bunch altogether couldn't get up enough nerve to scare a rabbit."

I said, "I'm afraid Bill's right. Too shiftless even to get out of the sun. Only thing they're good at is makin' kids."

CHAPTER
15

We sat around after grub in a grim and daunsy silence, none of us having any cheer to offer. I knew Barbona didn't think Mark stood much chance of driving Tolliver and his sheep off Bar B Cross grass, at least not before they'd eaten it. I wasn't that confident. After what he'd done here I'd not put it past him to fire his own range, buildings and all, if that was what it took.

I couldn't think why, but the way I had him figured was that better than half of what he was doing was dust thrown up to obscure some hidden purpose. Sure he meant to grab every bit of range he could but this, to my notion, was not his prime concern. Marrying Terry must be a means to whatever he had in mind.

He had the men and guns to take over her range whether she married him or not. Yet consider the horrible things he had done in a brutal attempt to coerce her. To me it was fury, not madness, that was back of his crazy antics, a cold determination to have his way regardless.

He'd become a man you balked at gravest peril.

What all of us wanted right now more than anything was to get this feud or whatever it was stopped before things got any worse. The big question was *how*. And to me, with so much hanging over us, it looked like being beyond our power.

The trail Bar B Cross men had used getting up here before came up from below and around the far side of the corrals where I had my horses. And those horses, after the nature of their kind, would set up a racket if Mark's bunch tried to surprise us by that means again.

Just the same, in my jittery frame of mind, I sent Terry's tough Texican with the smashed hand out to keep watch, confident he'd reason enough to stay awake. If the occasion presented itself he might not hit anything, but using his good hand he could sure as hell pull the trigger to alert us.

That tended to I went back to my thinking, and at last I managed to latch on to something. From a hopeless future I began to draw hope. The next hour I spent going over the parts and attempting to fit them together, trying to figure how to work it.

Seemed to me I would need two helpers and one of them straightaway. First I'd better have a talk with Edwardo, and on the heels of that I'd have to habla with Barbona. So, two birds with one ride.

With the excuse of checking yet again the whereabouts of what sheep we had left, I went off to throw my saddle on one of the finished horses I'd been used to keeping in the barn. It didn't take me over half an hour to locate Terry's woollies and, as expected, the Navajo kid was with them.

"Edwardo," I said, "I've got a little chore for you. Reckon you can get a line on where Elder is, sneak up on that outfit without them knowing?"

"You bet," he grunted, obviously pleased.

"Go ahead then. I'll get one of the Yaquis to take over here. Now, just in case you're discovered snooping, you tell them you've come to tip them off that Barbona's Yaquis are planning a surprise attack and a big cow killing. Got it?"

"They won't see me."

"So much the better. All right then, take off."

I found Barbona without too much bother and told him I'd borrowed his herder. He nodded. "Dogs'll keep 'em bunched. What's on your mind?"

"Some rannies make a living huntin' wild horses—you know how they work?"

"So?"

"They've a trick of securin' particularly desirable critters. Reckon you could do it?"

The man was reputed to be a crack shot. That he was also a rogue I knew from firsthand acquaintance. "Sure," he said like he wondered if I still had all my marbles. "No big deal if I was hankerin' to be satisfied with that sort."

"Think you could do the same trick with a man?"

He considered scuffed boots, peered up at me sharply. "You serious?"

Nodding, I told him what I had in mind. "I ain't interested in morals," Terry's boss of Yaquis declared with a snort, "only cash."

"If you accept this job you may be doin' yourself out of some."

Our bandit grinned. "Not likely. Expert service comes high these days. What you figure to do with him?"

"When you've a need to know you'll be told. I'll be in touch," I said, and pointed my horse at a walk toward the house, trying to decide how to refine my notion a bit more. Another essential element, of course, involved using Terry and this part, if it didn't go off like clockwork, looked like being the riskiest angle of the whole affair. Best, I thought, to keep her in the dark, for if she knew what I was up to she might in self-consciousness give the show away.

I had to anti-godle around a bit to keep the corraled horses from setting up an alarm. I therefore made my approach to the house in a roundabout fashion, coming in from the north instead of from the west as I'd left it. Even so, I hadn't yet got into the yard when Dude Inman's nerved-up voice jumped at me from a corner of the forge shop: "Stop right there an' put a name to yourself, bucko!"

"Relax," I muttered. "It's just me, Gracious Gill."

"Come up where I can get a look at you. . . . That's far enough. Strike a light."

I scraped a match across a pants leg and cupping it showed my face.

Inman laughed. "Advance, friend. How are the sheep?"

Edwardo returned just after noon of the following day. "You find him?"

The Navajo nodded. "Sheep all over his yard and the sheepmen have taken over the ranch house. Elder's holed up at the Rock Springs line camp."

"Good," I said. "Now get back to the Yaquis and tell Barbona I want him up here on the double."

The Rock Springs line camp of the Bar B Cross was not over ten miles from the O'Brian doorstep. When our hired bandido rode in I said, "Rock Springs. I'm going to loan you this army telescope. I want you to get over in that neighborhood and scout out a good place for us to work from, and find out, if you can, how much of a crew he's got there. These hills run almost over to those springs so you can stay out of sight if you're careful—an' you better be. I don't want this stunt knocked hell west an' crooked," I added with a scowl.

Piki gave me a mocking grin. "What d'you reckon I did before I had you around to advise me? Duck soup—nothin' to it. That's a game I kin play with the best of 'em."

"Get over there now, and if the signs are right we'll pull this off tomorrow."

With a lift of the hand he turned his horse and departed.

"What's up?" Bill Hazel stepped out from behind the bunkhouse. "What you two been augurin' about?"

"Little chore he's taking off my hands. Tolliver's taken over Elder's headquarters and Mark and his outfit are at Rock Springs."

"You reckon he's fixing to hit us again?"

"Not right soon, I wouldn't think. Reckon he's got enough on his plate for the moment trying to figure how to rid his ranch of Tolliver's woollies."

Hazel said, "By what I saw of Tolliver that's easier said than done, I'd imagine."

"I'd like to think so. How's Reb's hand?"

"Don't look too good to me. All swelled up an' discolored."

"He ought to ride into town and have the doc look at it."

"What I told him. Just wasted breath," Hazel said disgustedly. "He keeps foolin' around he's like to lose it."

I found Lockhart in the sitting room staring out the window. There wasn't no doubt the man was in intense pain. Even the tight-drawn skin of his face looked gray. "No thanks," he said when I offered to ride in with him. "I'm not havin' no sawbones whack off my fingers!"

"Better the fingers than the whole damn hand."

"I'll make out," he growled, stubborn as a mule.

But next morning when Terry took the bandage off there were angry red streaks edging up the back of his hand. Terry peered at it aghast. "You're going to town, Reb Lockhart, if we have to carry you there!"

We finally got him onto a horse and both Terry and I rode in with him. Since we'd started early we reached Four

Corners a little after nine and were lucky enough to find the doc home. The doc came out after about ten minutes. "No use you folks waiting. I've got to take off that hand. Be a couple days before he's fit to ride." He regarded us gravely. "Might even be a week."

Terry's face went pale but she said to send the bill to the Circle Dot. We went outside and started for home. "I feel terrible," she said. "We should have made him come in sooner. I don't know what he'll ever do without that hand."

I guessed he would have to be fitted with a hook, and wondered what he'd said, knowing the doc would have questioned Reb about it. I reckoned he had probably refused to talk about it. Be just like him. It was the Texas way.

CHAPTER
16

By the time we got back to the ranch the clouds had waggled on out of the sky, the sun beamed down like it was filled with Old Crow, and on the porch Terry's mother had liked to describe as "the verandah" Piki Barbona perched like a bird of prey, darkly waiting.

The others were hunkered down where the bunkhouse threw enough shade to squat in, Hazel idly scratching pictures on the hardpan, Inman earnestly munching on his cud of Picnic Twist. Both looked the question neither cared to ask, and Terry said, tight-faced, "Doc's keeping him there till he gets over the shock."

Barbona got up with his vulture's grin to opine it was time they got moving if they were going to.

Terry's head came around to probe my face. "What's he talking about?"

"Got something he wants to show us," I said. I turned to Barbona and said, "We're ready. You want those boys to traipse along, too?"

Barbona, swiveling a look at them, shook his head, climbed aboard his horse and led off, pointing west. Terry, still eyeing me curiously, kneed her mount after him with me falling in beside her. "What's going on?" she wanted to know.

I said with a shrug, "You'll see when we get there."

During the course of that ride I recalled how most of my efforts to mislead Ace Jolly had barked up the wrong tree, and my attempt to set the cow crowd at odds had only served to push Ace further under Mark Elder's thumb. And how that futile trek to the reservation had turned out such a waste of time and energy when, had I stayed at home, Reb Lockhart might still have had both hands and Terry's mother . . .

I clenched my jaws on the knowledge that regrets never buttered any parsnips, and dismally wondered if this would wind up being another of my blunders. It could all come to nothing or even backfire against us, and I still had to broach Terry's part in this stratagem, a part she might refuse to have anything to do with.

She did not, I knew, have my devious type of mind. Her notions pretty generally traveled a straight line, subterfuge and chicanery being foreign to her nature. If she rebelled against the part assigned her, refused to play the judas goat, I was going to be left holding another goddamn busted flush. And I was increasingly afraid—now that we were down to the nuts and bolts of this operation—she would give me a withering look and head for home.

I wished now I hadn't thought of it, not wanting her to think the less of me and just about convinced, regardless of possible benefits, she would take the view the end I sought did not justify the means.

We were dropping now with increased caution off higher ground and into the foothills flanking the flats. We could see a lot of Bar B Cross cattle and off, perhaps a mile beyond, the outlines of Elder's Rock Springs cabin. With pulses quickening I was unable to find more than one horse tied there, which seemed to indicate its out-of-sight rider must be there by himself.

Barbona, pulling up to get out the glass I had loaned him and focus it, said over his shoulder in a pleased sort of mutter, "Crew must be off tryin' to dislodge Tolliver. If it's Elder's horse standin' front of that shack—"

He broke off with a curse as three mounted men larruped up to the cabin. Mark appeared in the doorway, glaring. We were too far off to hear what was said, could not even hear their voices. "You ready," Barbona asked, glancing at Terry.

So we'd finally arrived at the moment of truth.

"Haven't told her yet," I said gruffly and, turning to Terry, said, "I can't see but one way we'll ever get this thing stopped; so long as Mark's loose there'll be more killin'. What we've come here to do is take him out of it."

She stared at me whitely. "You mean *kill* him? You've come here to bushwhack him?"

"Nothing so drastic as that. What I got in mind is to get him away from his hardcase crew, take him out of circulation till we can get this thing ironed out."

A little of the fierceness fell out of her look. "Oh. You want to make him a prisoner—kidnap him?" When I nodded, she said, "Where do I come into it?"

"I figure if he sees you he'll come tearin' after you, away from the guns he's got on his payroll. What we want you to do is to let him discover you, with no visible protection, apparently on your way home from someplace."

"And then you'll pounce on him?"

"What we want you to do," Barbona cut in, "is to ride along the edge of them flats. You see where that brush is off to the left mebbe half a mile? Just back of it's a trail that comes up through the hills in the direction of your place. We want him to figure that's what you're aimin' for."

"Suppose he doesn't come after me?"

Piki grinned. "Don't worry about that. He'll come after you all right. When he gets near enough you'll discover him and stop. Let him come up to you. That's when we nail him."

She eyed Barbona a pretty good while—three, four moments anyway—before saying coldly bitter, "What you're wanting me to do is trap him."

"Well," I reluctantly admitted, "that's one way of seein' it. On the other hand, do you know any surer way of stopping whatever he's up to?"

"I wish I did," she said, shaking her head. Those shocked and bitter eyes jerked again to Barbona. "What if the whole bunch comes larruping after me?"

"Be too surprised," I pointed out. "Only Mark—happens he sees you at the edge of those flats barreling along tryin' to get onto that trail—will have any reason to take out after you. When you pretend to discover him comin' hell-bent an' he pulls up beside you . . . that's when we knock him out of the saddle."

"How? I can't see him cooperating—"

"Won't have no choice," Barbona assured her. "What I'm goin' t' do is crease him—knock him out with a bullet, like his outfit done with Inman. Just get him over there, I'll do the rest. Come on, let's git started before he goes ridin' off with them others."

I tried to will her into acceptance. It brought her face around. "If he's killed I'll always feel guilty—"

"Killing him's the last thing we're wantin' right now."

"But you can't know . . ."

Barbona showed his tiger's grin. "Just takes a steady hand is all."

CHAPTER
17

The saturnine Piki had picked himself a commanding position behind a waist-high rock at the top edge of that brush where we could keep her in view all the time she was out there. A fold in the ground back of this served to hide our mounts from anyone below.

Shooting downhill had a distinct disadvantage, contributing to my disquiet, but I figured Barbona for enough experience to overcome this. If he should happen through misjudgment to terminate Mark it would be no more than the bastard had coming.

I did, however, want him alive awhile yet. This whole deal had been engineered to get Elder's John Henry on a bill of particulars that would prove him the aggressor and absolve the rest of us.

It had taken Terry about twenty minutes to get onto flat ground, but she was out there now. We could see her plainly, loping toward our covert, and Mark suddenly rigid peering in her direction. Through the glass I could see his snarling features as he flung himself aboard to send his horse hurtling after her.

Though I could see she was playing her part to perfection,

leading him on like a shill at a crap table, I was scared she might panic and not let him come up with her or put it off too long. But there . . .

She'd pulled up, and him alongside her reaching for her bridle.

Barbona's gun went off. I saw Mark lurch and tumble out of the saddle. Dragging our horses we went scrabbling through brush in a sweat to get hold of him, discovering Terry, bone white, peering down at him in horror.

"Have you killed him?" she cried in a jumpety voice.

Barbona, snorting, hauled the man off the ground and flung the limp shape facedown across his saddle. "Jesus!" he muttered. "Bad news!" Looking up I spied the rest of Elder's bunch—the ones we'd seen at the line camp—flogging our way and practically upon us.

Cursing in a passion I whacked Terry's horse across the rump to get it started. No time now to tie Mark on with lead plums buzzing round us like hornets. Nothing for it but to barrel off without him. I could hardly see straight I was in such a pelter at having all this go for naught, but I wasn't fool enough to stay there and be clobbered.

The only blessed thing to come out of the whole affair was that those Bar B Cross hellions were too busy farting round with Mark to think of coming after us.

When we were well away from them Terry asked what I'd have done had we succeeded in getting him away from his outfit. I hadn't gone much into that part of it beyond intending to hold him until we'd some way got him to admit on paper his responsibility for her mother's death and Lockhart's smashed hand and his scheme by force to dispossess us smaller owners.

She said, "I doubt you'd have done it without torture. We'd have had him on our hands forever I'm afraid."

"And what's wrong with torture?" Barbona scoffed. "I know a few tricks would have loosened him up!"

She gave him a disgusted look and sent her mount skittering out ahead of us.

"Touchy, ain't she?" Barbona laughed. "Life ain't ever been comfortable enough for most of us to feel that squeamish. Reckon she'd never believe the things I been through."

I guessed he was right. "You made a damn fine shot. Too bad we had to waste it."

He looked back a few times but saw nothing to alarm him.

"What's your next move?" he asked finally.

"Don't know." I was still some way from getting over that one. To have come so close and have it washed down the drain wasn't something a man got over in five or ten minutes. I couldn't rid myself of temper, kept going over it time and again without seeing how we could have done any different. To have stayed back there long enough to have roped him onto that horse would damn sure have got me killed.

There was a mighty sharp difference between boldness and being foolhardy. Graveyards were filled with folks who hadn't noticed.

I didn't reckon Mark likely to guess what we'd been up to. Probably figured we'd tried to kill him; I hadn't a doubt he'd understand that. I didn't expect it to alter his plans much. I guessed he'd bull on ahead with them come hell or high water.

But I couldn't think what he'd be like to do next.

A couple days later we found out what he'd done. A passing Indian had told one of the Yaquis who'd passed it on to Barbona who'd ridden up to tell me. Seemed Mark's crew of hardcases had raided the greasy-sackers, the little one-man outfits, driven them off their land, and what they hadn't torn down they'd left burning.

So we'd get no help there. I hadn't thought we would anyway.

I guessed I'd better find out what was going on at my place.

Accordingly I threw my hull on Surefoot and was about to set off when Bill Hazel insisted he go along with me. We set off about the middle of the afternoon. I'd figured we'd not have to get near enough to find ourselves trapped in case Mark's bunch or Jolly had seen fit to move in.

Turned out it was lucky we hadn't elected to slip down there at night. From a wooded rise a bit north of the buildings we could tell the place was occupied, and before very long we discovered which bunch had taken it over. No occasion for guesswork once we'd seen Ace Jolly.

We were still up there watching when Elder rode up from the flats with his Bar B Cross foreman, a hard-jawed fellow by the name of Vance Ullbrack. They pulled up just out of earshot to habla awhile with the obsequious Jolly. All three of them then went back to the house, and pretty soon Mark rode back into sight accompanied by Jolly, also mounted.

"What you reckon they're up to?"

"Don't know," I said, "but maybe if we sort of tag along back of them we'll be able to find out."

CHAPTER
18

Had Barbona been with me I might have taken another stab at taking Mark out of this, but I couldn't see either Hazel or me bouncing slugs off his skull without permanent injury. And I couldn't, unfortunately, set out to deliberately kill an old friend . . . at least a man I'd grown up considering my friend. Even believing Mark Elder had no such scruples could not prod me into doing it.

I take no particular pride in such squeamishness. There's a heap of things about me I have never understood. You'd have thought by this time I'd have grown out of my finicking notions and the deviousness that for twenty-three years had kept me intact without visible blemish.

One thing I could do a lot better than most. It's been said I could track a fly across bare rock which, of course, is preposterous; I'd never had much trouble reading sign, and it came to me now we might follow those buggers and perhaps find out a thing or two.

We let them get clean out of sight before taking after them. And pretty soon it was plain they were bending their steps in the direction of Terry's headquarters.

It occurred to me if we set them afoot we might be able to

collar them. "Let's get a bit nearer and see how it looks."

So we stepped up our pace and damn near ran up on them. A pair of blue whistlers passing too close for comfort got us off their tracks in one hell of a hurry.

When I'd time to think clearly I felt fairly sure they'd lost no time hustling away from the sound of those shots themselves, having been at that point scarcely a mile from Terry's doorstep.

Both she and Dude were in the brush with rifles when Hazel and I rode into the yard. "Expect they've cleared out," I told her questioning look.

Inman asked, "Who were you sniping at?"

Bill Hazel said, "That was Elder an' Jolly. We'd been tagging along to see what they were up to and we just about run over them. It was them done the shootin', not us."

"Probably," I told her, "they were aimin' to see how you were set up for company. Might be figurin' to pay us another visit. I don't reckon this place'll be healthy for a spell. I think we ought to get Piki and his Yaquis an' pull back a ways, let 'em think we've left."

I could see the speculation in the slant of her green eyes. "What about my sheep?"

"Don't believe they're much on his mind any longer. I think you can leave them to Edwardo and Barbona's dogs."

She said, "I can't understand Mark leaving his headquarters overrun with Tolliver's sheep."

"Except he's got bigger fish to fry. Anyway I don't think he's able to drive Tolliver out; likely figures once the grass is gone Tolliver will take his sheep someplace else, which of course he'll have to. That's how I'd see it if I was in his boots. He's probably countin' on the sheriff to get rid of Tolliver."

"After what he did to those greasy-sackers I wouldn't

think he could count on much help from the law."

"Sheriff was elected to serve the big owners. He'll not shed many tears over that bunch of squatters. I think what we're about to see here is Ace Jolly with a part of Mark's crew taking another whack at what sheep you've got left, the idea being to make enough racket to pull any help you've got here down there to fight them off, giving Mark a free hand to come in with the rest of his outfit and take this place over."

"Sounds logical to me," Bill Hazel said grimly.

"Then," Terry said, and I could see she didn't like it, "where's the sense in letting him think this place is up for grabs?"

"There's higher ground back of these buildings. If we dig in up there with Piki's rifles we can blast that bunch into doll rags."

"Don't you care what happens to your Navajo—that boy you're fixing to leave with my sheep?"

"Edwardo's old enough to know what the score is. He's not goin' to make any target of himself."

She said with those green eyes hard on my face, "That brain wave you had for capturing Mark didn't work out the way you figured. If you're wrong about this—"

"I might be," I admitted. "The four of us couldn't hold this place anyway against the combined strength of Mark and Jolly. Between 'em they've got more than a dozen men if they throw the whole works at us. The big reason, I think, why Mark doesn't go after Tolliver is he's scared if hard pressed Tolliver will burn the place down."

She said angrily, "And what's to prevent me doing the same?"

"I don't think he gives a whoop for your buildings."

It was plain she didn't care for that remark either. She gave a distracted glance at Dude Inman then slapped her stare back onto my face. "Then what *is* he after?"

"If I could answer that I'd have the key to this whole business. It's what I been askin' myself night an' day. The only thing I can think is that there's something about this spread that, to his mind, puts a premium on it. First he tries, through you, to marry it. When you balked he tried threats. Right now I think he's decided to go whole hog and take it away from you."

"Then he'll have to do it over my dead body!"

"I believe he's prepared to if nothing else works. Considerable blood gets spilled in a range feud. Who's to say you didn't catch a stray bullet?"

She apparently found that hard to swallow.

"You're still regarding him as someone you've known all your life. He's no longer that man, not inside anyway. I made the same mistake till he told me point blank where I'd get off if I crossed him. So now he's got Ullbrack moved onto my place. One way or another he means to move onto this one." I looked at her grimly. "You better believe it."

CHAPTER
19

My words seemed to have changed the whole shape of things for her. It was obviously hard for her to accept my prediction, but I guessed I had finally managed to get through to her. Perhaps it was remembrance of what had happened to her mother and what he'd done to Reb's hand that presently convinced her. I thought she looked like someone rudely awakened from deep sleep. It was in that sort of fashion that she nodded her head.

"All right," I said, "let's get on with it. Dude, you go fetch Barbona and his Yaquis. No tellin' when he'll hit us but it's like to be right soon. If he catches us here we'll be sitting ducks. Bill, you an' me," I told Hazel, "had better keep our eyes peeled till Piki gets up here."

Terry went silently into the house. At the corral I roped out a horse for her and saddled it. I sure hated having to leave my horses here after all the efforts I'd been to trying to make sure he wouldn't get hold of them. But right now was no time to be thinking about horses.

It was probably seeing those buggers inside the chain links of that expensive fence that had screwed me up to this pitch of turmoil, for I was mostly damn careful to sit

on my temper, battening it down, not allowing it to shove
me into dangerous confrontations. Even in the thwarted
attempt to make off with Mark I'd been the manipulator,
not the aggressor. Brawling had ever been foreign to my
nature.

I wanted to get out of here before something irreversible
caught up with me.

In a fine sweat of impatience I got to thinking it might
be a deal smarter to take along some of my horses for extras
in case we had to make a run for it. I shouted for Terry to
get a wiggle on, caught up in my concept of what could
happen, and became so worked up I very nearly bolted
when I caught the sound of approaching hoofs.

Turned out to be only Hazel with Barbona and the Yaquis
I'd sent for, yet even their presence did little to reassure
me. Terry came out with a rifle and climbed into her saddle
and I led off at once. "You leavin' them horses?" Barbona
yelled at me. I was beset with such fluster I didn't even
look round.

Not until we topped out on a wooded rim high above
the Circle Dot buildings was I able to get myself in hand.
From this height, despite the encroaching dusk, we could
see the whole layout, even the gray huddle of distant sheep;
and I thought to myself that Terry's old man when he
built his headquarters should have chosen this commanding
position.

We were safely out of rifle range here, with no chance
of being caught unawares. I was able to shake off the
apprehensions that had nagged at me and get my mind
dug out of cold storage. It was time I did some serious
thinking and nobody knew this better than myself.

The stars seemed close as night closed round us. On some
distant ridge a coyote yammered and, except for that and
the tinkle of spur chains and saddle squeak, a vast stillness

surrounded us. "What do we do now?" Piki's gruff voice was impatient.

"Be quiet," I said, "and let me think."

To know what to do with any chance of success I first had to know what was in Mark's mind, what was driving the man to these outrageous acts. And I was as far from knowing that as I'd ever been. Until I could find some plausible notion I would have to go on trying to play it by ear, a hit-or-miss system I direly mistrusted.

I recalled my remark about blasting them to doll rags. It wasn't like to be that easy. To keep any control at all over Piki, his volatile nature must be given something to do. Only the prospect of imminent violence could hold such a fellow long in check. I told him to leave his horses up here and slip down with his boys and spread them out within good rifle range of the house and keep watch for Mark's crowd. "I'll give long odds they'll be here before sun-up. They're going to think we've cleared out and get careless. We don't want them dug in. Anytime you see movement put a blue whistler through it."

"How about burning out that Rock Springs line camp?"

"Good thinking." I nodded. "Send one of the Yaquis."

After they'd gone, slipping off into the shadows silent as wolves, Terry wanted to know, "Are we going to sit here all night?"

Barbona's Rock Springs suggestion had given me a new direction. Though I'd been listening intently for sound of Mark's arrival, I'd caught no indication of this when lamplight showed from the windows of Terry's house. "They've come!" she muttered.

"And we'll be leavin'," I said. "Come along, and be quiet as you can till we get off this point."

Not giving any of them time for questions, I turned

Surefoot at once and struck off at a walk, angling down
the back side of this high spot in a roundabout fashion that
would keep us well clear of the Circle Dot headquarters.
We heard the occasional crack of a rifle above the clump
of our horses' hoofs and twenty minutes later I swung onto
the trail that led past my fence on the way to the flats. My
place was dark as I led the way past it, pulling up a hundred
yards or so below.

"Bill," I told Hazel, "I'm going to leave you here to take
care of Ullbrack if he's still around. We'll pick you up on
the way back. I think we'll do a heap better just nibblin'
at them than bein' caught up in any full-scale shoot-out."

Discovering I was heading for the flats and Jolly's range
and the improvements he'd put in by way of tanks and
windmills, Terry wanted to know what was up my sleeve.
She said, "You're not, I hope, planning to topple those
mills?"

I told her I didn't figure to do that.

She twisted her head to eye me suspiciously. Inman said
with a grin, "I expect we're about to pay Jolly a visit."

"That's right," I told them. "Turnabout is fair play by
my way of reckoning. While he's enjoying himself chasing
your sheep we'll drop in and make it cost him a little."

"I want to know what you're letting me in for!"

"Nothing to get in a stew about," I said. "All you've got
to do is hang on to our horses."

The moon was up now and showed Jolly's home place
about a mile ahead of us.

"This won't hurt him as much as I would like for it to,
but he's going to find it plenty inconvenient."

"You're going to fire his buildings—burn him out!"

"Right on the money," I said to Inman. "Give the lady
that baby-doll."

"Don't you realize," she demanded, "you'll be laying us open to reprisals?"

"He's already slaughtered half your sheep. Don't you want to get back at him?"

"But there's nobody home—"

"All the better," I said as we drew rein in the yard. "This won't take long. I figured his bunch would be up there with Mark. Hang on to our horses."

"I'll take the out-buildin's," Dude said as I ran up on the porch, and went inside through the unlocked door. Since the place didn't have any curtains I gathered up every scrap of loose paper, all the stuff from his desk, and piled the whole mess up against an inner wall, and during a moment of fearful uncertainty touched a match to it. For a man of my temperament, an act of extreme recklessness.

For several moments I stood queerly fascinated before the enormity of what I'd done. Every ingrown instinct adamantly urged me to stamp out those flames. Memory of Terry's shocked tones and look pushed me toward them. There still was time to undo this mischief, this open act of manifest villainy.

Instead I eyed the flames defiantly and with a mirthless laugh stepped out into the night, not even bothering to shut the door.

At last I'd gotten outside myself. Instead of my cautious maneuvering of others I'd finally managed to stand up and be counted. Heady stuff and intensely frightening to a man who had always kept himself out of trouble. I laughed again with a crazy satisfaction.

CHAPTER
20

Terry appeared to be eyeing me curiously when I rejoined her and Inman, but I gave this no thought, being suddenly cognizant of the complete lack of light out there in the direction of the Bar B Cross line camp, which one of the Yaquis was supposed to have fired. Had this been done, even eight miles away across these flats it should have been plainly visible. Had Piki for some reason changed his mind or found no chance? Did the cow crowd have the Yaquis pinned down?

We were too far away to catch the sound of rifles. I could not believe that engagement was resolved. Looking back at Jolly's flaming buildings I had an overpowering desire to strike again.

Bringing my attention back to Inman, I was startled when Terry, reaching out to touch me, said, "What's come over you tonight? Why are you suddenly getting into this personally?"

"Don't you think I've as much to lose as you if Mark comes out on top in this ruckus?" When she didn't say anything I put my look back on Inman, figuring by now Bill Hazel would have taken care of Ullbrack. "Take Terry up to my place and wait for me—"

"Aren't you coming with us?" Terry asked, leaning toward me, eyes intently probing my face. I don't know what she could see with the moon now deeply into the west. When I shook my head, she said, "Haven't you done enough for one night?" She sounded worried, I thought; could she possibly care?

She'd never given me reason to think she considered me more than a friend.

"I've a little more business to attend to first, but I'll be up there soon as I can, and we'll go find out what has happened at your place. Go on. Get whackin'."

Dude Inman said, "Supposin' Hazel's not in charge at your place? That foreman of Mark's ain't no pushover."

"Then use your best judgment." I swung Surefoot away before they thought up more objections, determined to get on with what I had in mind.

The moon sank lower as I rode toward Rock Springs. It had seemed to me, and still did, that by destroying Jolly's base and this line camp of Mark's, he might be more inclined to turn his attention toward liberating his home place from Tolliver's sheep and give us a breathing spell.

In any event, now that I'd broken out of my shell and liked the feel of it, I was minded to show him I was still in this fracas and no longer to be taken for granted. Any hurt I could deal him would be that much gained.

I thought some more about Terry and wondered if I really had any kind of chance with her. I had always figured, as no doubt Mark had, that any interest in me so far as she was concerned went no further than a tolerant friendship. And that was probably true, but now that I'd flung myself into open contention perhaps her feelings might change toward me. Leastways it was something to hope for.

The place was still standing when I got to Mark's camp, no sign in the grayness of false dawn that any of Piki's

Yaquis had been anywhere near it. I'd probably find a lamp or two I could use to speed destruction. A couple horses nickered at me from the corral out back. I rode over there and turned them loose, even took the time to chase them away, since fire has the habit of scaring horses silly.

Having done this good deed with the hope of obtaining a star for my crown I rode back to the cabin, prepared to find the lamp or lamps so nearly empty as made little difference. But the first thing I saw as I stepped over the threshold was the sprawled dead shape of one of our Yaquis.

As I stood there in shock Mark's familiar voice said, "Just unbuckle that gun belt almighty careful."

CHAPTER
21

He was somewhere back of me out of my sight. I had not expected to find anyone here, particularly not him, but this was no excuse for invading his property empty-handed. Unbuckling my shell belt, gun still holstered, despite a temptation I let it drop, not compounding my folly with a second mistake.

"Step inside and make like that Injun facedown on the floor."

With no choice that wasn't suicide I grudgingly complied.

I heard the approach of bootsteps. He said conversationally, "One false move is all you'll get," and I was ready to believe it. "Was it you that set Jolly's place afire?"

I said, "Yeah," and felt the thud of his boot against my ribs.

"You ungrateful bastard. Cross them hands behind you."

It looked like I had run out of choices.

He said, after tying my wrists with a piggin' string, "I expect Ace Jolly will be wanting a few words with you. Get up on your feet." I got another taste of his boot. "Every game has its rules. When I say frog, you jump—savvy?"

When you're lying facedown with your hands tied behind you, it is considerably more difficult to get up than you'd imagine. Boots, I found, are a wonderful persuader. When presently I stood facing him, this son of a bitch said, "All right, frog, get over in that corner and stand there till I say different."

He went over to the stove and built up a fire and proceeded to fry up a mess of already refried beans. I watched him pick up a battered blue graniteware coffeepot, scoop up some water from the tank at the back, throw in some Arbuckle's and put it on to boil. When all was ready and the cabin filled with agonizing smells, he sat down at the scarred table and with three or four biscuits went about the business of filling his gut.

He sat on awhile after this performance, presently got out his Durham, and built up a smoke while looking me over with a calculating stare. The sound of hoofs pulled up outside with a grumble of voices, and Ace Jolly came in with two of his punchers. "Did you know some bastards burnt—"

Jolly got that far when his mean little eyes fell on me. Staring bug-eyed, his mouth dropped open. "Not bastards"— Mark smiled—"just the one you're lookin' at."

Jolly drew in his breath, swelling up like a carbuncle. Three strides took his leaf-lard shape around the table to pull up before me with his shaved-hog face gone as dark as thunder. His fist lashed out and slammed me into the wall and, not satisfied with that, he fetched me another. When the next one landed I went out like a light.

Next thing I knew Mark was hauling me onto my feet again. "I told you to stand," he said wickedly, and when I sagged against the wall he doubled me over with a fist in my stomach, brought a knee up into my face like a hammer, and after that I lost track of things.

When finally I got my eyes open again there was blood in my mouth and the whole front of my face was one horrible ache. "Get up off that floor!" Mark's voice shouted. His boot thudded into me with calculated savagery.

Somehow I got onto my feet.

"Don't let me see you slumped down again."

He turned away from me then and said to somebody else, "You'll find a length of chain out in the forge shop. Go make a pair of shackles and fasten 'em onto it. Give a yell when they're ready and we'll fetch him over there."

I didn't pass out again, but it was some while I reckon before I was able to take in my surroundings. Three of Mark's hard-faced hands were between me and the door, making sure I didn't leave, not that I felt in any shape to. "Pretty specimen; ain't he?" one of them said to the others. "Don't see how they can bang him up any worse without cripplin' him permanent."

One of the other rannies said, "Prob'ly will before they're through with him."

The third hombre said with a nasty grin, "Shouldn't wonder but what the boss has got a few things in mind for him."

"If Jolly was runnin' this," the first speaker said, "he'd be hangin' head down over a fire by now."

Mark's shouted voice called, "Fetch that arsonist over here."

With one of them grabbing hold of each arm I was hustled outside and through the blaze of a livid sun across the yard to the blacksmith shop, where they gave me a shove that sent me lurching inside to bring up against the anvil.

Someone cut the rope from my gone-to-sleep wrists. Someone else grabbed up one, slipped on a shackle and hammered it shut. I was spun around then and had one fastened to the other wrist. With three feet of heavy chain dangling between them I was sent staggering through the door. "Take him over to the tie rack," Mark said pleasantly. "Looks like he needs thawin' out a mite."

"Reckon this sun oughta do it," one of the others said happily.

"Knock up that rail so we can slide this chain over it," Mark said. When this was done someone hammered it down again, and Ace Jolly came up to me lugging one of those heavy weights generally used to anchor a buggy horse. This he dropped, unintentionally missing my foot by half an inch, looping the rope attached to it around my neck. "Guess that'll take care of him," he muttered with a vindictive smirk.

Mark said then, skewering me with a baleful stare, "We're going to try a little experiment, Gill. We're fixin' to discover how long a man can survive without grub or water. Have fun." He laughed and went off with the others to hunker down in the comparative coolness of the cabin's shade.

Where I was hitched in the broiling glare of that noontime sun it must have been at least a hundred and ten. They'd taken away my hat, and that hitching rack rail was just high enough to keep my butt off the ground by about three inches. I could manage to kneel, but ten minutes of that was more than plenty. I could either stand erect or lean against the rail, and already groggy the furnace heat of that sun soon had me light-headed.

When the landscape began to go round and round I shut my eyes, but this was no help at all against the heat, which wasn't due to abate for a long five hours, at which time in this season that brassy ball in the sky should be nearing the western peaks.

My throat was dry and I could feel the sweat trickling down my back, down cramped arms, down my nose, into my eyes and off my chin. If I didn't get sunstroke it would be a howling wonder. My nose was probably broken, I'd lost a couple teeth from the smash of Mark's knee after he'd doubled me over, and my head ached abominably. If I didn't pass out I guessed I'd go crazy. It was the thought of my weight depending from shackled wrists that kept me conscious.

The hours dragged with unbelievable torture, but at last the six men sent one of their number inside the cabin to cook up some supper, and when he sang out the rest of them trooped in and I was left in my misery to eye the black shapes of circling buzzards.

Mark, Jolly and three of the others presently came out, belched a couple times, then went over to the corral, where they roped out and saddled the available horses, Mark swinging aboard the one the sixth man had come on.

Leaving his companions he cut over to have a look at me. "Still sweatin'? I'm astonished. You're holdin' up better'n I figured. I've left a man here to keep an eye on you. If it looks like you're about to get loose he's got orders to shoot."

When I didn't say anything he kneed his horse nearer and gave me another boot in the ribs. "I've fixed up a quitclaim deed to your place, all it needs is your John Henry. You ready to sign?"

I didn't have enough spit left to talk with.

"You'll stay right where you are till you do," he said, and with a laugh rode off after the others.

CHAPTER
22

After a while the man left behind came out with a rifle and settled himself with his back to the cabin wall.

The worst of the heat had gone with the sun, but my head and face gave me more fits than ever and my legs were numb from the knees on down. My wrists were raw from the blacksmithed shackles and I guessed I'd likely be shivering soon, for the temperature these nights could take an astonishing dive.

Both Terry and Inman knew I'd set out for this camp. It was remembrance of that which had kept me going through this terrible day. But suddenly as dusk thickened round me I saw my situation as Mark must have seen it. He hadn't left that ranny to make sure I stayed hitched; he'd been left to put a bullet in me at the first indication I was about to be rescued.

Despite the scrape of that rope round my neck the leeway I had for movement was scarcely more than twenty inches—not enough by half if that bugger started shooting. It was the most worrying notion I'd had all day and one not easily put aside.

Last night I'd figured my devious nature could be laid

to an excess of caution, from being afraid to let myself
go. Now that I could see where boldness had taken me I
tremendously longed to be back in my shell, wishing I'd
never tried to be different.

With night closing in a cold wind sprang up, but not cold
enough to stop time in its tracks. To my shivering thoughts
one thing seemed certain. Any attempt at a rescue could
mean my finish; I was only surprised I'd not seen this
before.

As the minutes ticked by, all too fast for me now, the
shape of my guard grew harder to make out against the
black blob of that cabin. In the gravelike quiet locking
me in with my thoughts I could detect no sound beyond
the chirping of crickets. Then my straining ears caught the
crunch of boots as my jailer got up and went into the cabin.
While I toyed with the notion he had gone for a coat, I
thought I heard at some distance the faint *crack crack* of
rifles, the imagined pulsation of hard-running horses.

Lamplight blossomed in the cabin window and that
damned bar of light traveled across twenty yards to set
me up as a perfect target. I heard the crunch of boots again
as the guard's black shape crossed the light and vanished
as he took up his former place against the wall.

The onrushing rumble of hoofs I'd imagined was now all
too real and indisputably coming this way. I could picture
Mark's man lifting rifle to shoulder . . .

Just as I felt sure he was about to fire the far sound of
those horses changed direction and went veering away, and
I sagged against the rail, weak and dizzy with relief.

If I could get through this night without being riddled I
promised myself I would make no further trouble for Mark,
let him have my place and get out of the country. I could
see with an awful clarity that being a live coward was better
than being dead.

• • •

With my mind made up to be a model citizen I found myself wondering why Terry, Inman and the hired guns paid to look out for our interests had made no attempt to discover what had become of me. I could not put down an increasing resentment at being valued so little to be so quickly forgotten. They probably thought I'd cleared out and, come to that, I wished I had.

I've no idea how long I dawdled with these notions. I jerked erect to a sudden gasp, which had seemed to come from the direction of the cabin. I couldn't see a thing with that light in my face. "Gotcha!" someone hissed through the sound of a falling body, and Barbona, striding into the light, said, "Hang on a bit longer an' I'll have you outa there," and went into the cabin and doused the lamp.

"We'd've got here sooner but we run into Mark's crowd—"

"How'd you know where I was?"

"Saw you through the glass when that numbskull lit the lamp." With the barrel of the guard's rifle he hammered the rail up and hauled me off it. "You're goin' to have to stand up."

"Can't do it," I grumbled as my knees buckled under me.

"No problem," he grunted, scooping me up and dropping me facedown across his saddle. "What happened to your horse?"

"Don't know. Wandered off maybe. Forgot all about him."

Hitching me over his shoulder he staggered into the forge shop and set me down alongside the anvil. He dug up a cold chisel and chopped off the chain. "Better leave them bracelets till we've got more time. This ain't no place to linger."

With one of my arms draped over his shoulder and one of his under it holding me upright, Piki muttered, "See if you can walk outa here," and, after a fashion the both of us managed to lurch over to his horse. "I'm goin' to put you in the saddle," he growled. "See if you kin stay there till I git up behind."

By clamping a hand round the horn I did, and he lost no time getting us away from there, heading for the brush where the trail up to my place wound through the hills. I was a bundle of aches from top to bottom, but the worst was my legs, which were no longer numb. I kept hold of the horn and he kept hold of me.

CHAPTER
23

We reached my place to find Bill Hazel and one of the Yaquis waiting, and Barbona got himself off the horse and I was able to get down by myself without falling. The others, I was told, had pushed on to the Circle Dot.

My nose was sore as a boil. I was having some difficulty getting breath through it, but contrary to previous thought it wasn't broken. Aside from being shy two front teeth and—thanks to Mark's knee—having a wrecked mouth, there wasn't, I reckoned, a lot wrong with me that rest wouldn't cure.

My house was still standing, and after I had staggered into it and Hazel got busy frying up some grub, I was glad to fall into a chair and stay there. I answered their questions in as few words as possible and told Piki about the dead Yaqui I'd found.

He said he'd lost another at Terry's last night, a plain case of carelessness. Mark had lost two and they'd dropped one of Jolly's. "So I guess," he said, "countin' that feller I potted at Rock Springs, we're not much worse or better off than before."

After we'd eaten I felt a mite better. "You oughta kept on your hat," Bill Hazel remarked with his eyes on my face, "that's a bad burn you got. Looks like to me you oughta be in bed."

So I let them persuade me.

When I got stiffly up and wandered into the kitchen again to discover Terry looking me over with evident concern, the lamps were still lit. I said, "How long have I been poundin' my ear and how'd you get here?"

"Twelve hours," Bill said. "I sent the Yaqui after her."

I put a hand gingerly up to my face. "Don't touch it," she said. "Your nose is badly swollen."

Hazel said, "You look like hell warmed over."

Which was how I felt, though I didn't mention it. "What's happened to your sheep an' my Navajo?"

She said, "The sheep are all right and so is Edwardo. One of the dogs was killed and we've two Yaquis left, one of them with a leg wound but still able to ride."

"Could have been worse," Bill Hazel opined. "You and Inman did a first-rate job on Jolly's place—ain't a thing left standin' but the main house chimney."

"What happened to Ullbrack?"

"Leaned again' a bullet," Hazel said cheerfully. "Between them, Elder an' Jolly ain't got but six hands left. They've been tryin' to dislodge Tolliver from Mark's headquarters without much luck, but they're still peckin' away at him."

"Has anyone found out how Reb's doing?"

Terry shook her head. "We're running low on grub. Someone's going to have to go to Four Corners and replenish our supplies."

"We're runnin' short of cartridges too," Hazel said.

"We could send Dude and one of the Yaquis with a couple of pack horses," I suggested, and Terry nodded. I said, "How are my horses?" and saw the quick look the pair of them exchanged. Hazel finally said, "I'm afraid Mark got away with them."

"Figures," I grumbled. "Let's get over there and get Dude on his way. It's gettin' light outside."

"Don't you think," Terry said, "you ought to get some more rest?"

"Ridin' will shake some of the stiffness out of me. Come on, let's get at it."

Walking our horses it was pretty near eight when we reached the Circle Dot.

Ten minutes later Dude Inman and the unwounded Yaqui with a couple of pack horses were on their way to Four Corners. We sent the wounded Yaqui up to the high ground back of the house with the glass I had loaned Piki.

Terry, I thought, was eyeing me anxiously. "Don't you think you'd better rest a bit?"

"And get all stiffened up again? I'm fine. I want to have another good look at your range. I want to know why Mark was so set, and apparently still is, on taking over this spread."

"Think there's gold on it?" Hazel asked with a grin.

"I doubt it, but there's somethin' here he seems to want mighty bad, and I think we ought to be lookin' for it."

"Then we'd better all look," Terry said, getting up.

"Who'll mind the store?" Barbona wanted to know.

"Your Yaqui with that glass can see all there is to look at. He can send up a smoke if we're needed," I told them.

So we all got mounted and set off on our search.

We spent five hours without turning up a thing and were now at the northernmost section of her land, the stretch nearest Villalobos, a grassless waste of stunted pear, rabbit brush and saguaros. Nothing but a rock-strewn hogback rose before us, a darker area showing across its center. I said to Hazel, "What's up there?"

"Just what you see, a mess of volcanic ash and clinkers."

"You ever been up there?"

"What's the use? You can see what it's like from here."

"But have you been up there?"

"I've ridden over it huntin' cows."

I said, "Let's take a look."

"Go ahead," Barbona said. "This horse needs a rest."

"Mine, too," Hazel grumbled.

"I'll go," Terry offered.

It proved a fairly rugged climb. I missed old Surefoot as we picked our way through the near-black rocks that looked like slag from a blast furnace. "According to Dad there was a lot of volcanic activity west of here when most of this land was under water," Terry mentioned. "About the time of the dynosaurs, I guess. I expect that accounts for this malapai."

Where we topped out the ground was relatively level, and up here there was more malapai; likewise a still standing but badly decayed saguaro looking ugly and leaking from its rotten insides. A sort of hunch grabbed hold of me, too vague right then to hold a great deal of meaning but convincing me of one thing.

I looked around intently.

"What is it? What do you see?" Terry asked, leaning toward me.

I said with a shrug, "The same thing you see." Which was true, so far as it went. There'd be no good telling her what I suspected. It wouldn't change anything to tell her that for my money this piece of ground was what Mark was after.

"Let's go," I said. "We better be getting back."

CHAPTER
24

She was looking at me oddly above a tight smile. "I think you've seen something you don't want to talk about."

"I haven't seen anything you haven't seen."

"Don't you feel you should confide in me?"

"All I've got is a pretty vague hunch concerned with what's put Mark on the warpath."

I found it hard to meet that questioning stare, but the whole notion of what I believed I'd latched on to was too outlandish and, if shared, might lead her to some wrong and dangerous conclusions. And I could be wrong. Her father had been all over this ground, and to say that this portion of it was what I reckoned was driving Mark to such outrageous actions could do her no good at all. One careless word from her could be a signed death warrant. Sometimes ignorance could be a real advantage, and from where I stood this looked like one of them.

Her look had changed. I thought to read a kind of resentment in the way she was eyeing me, a sort of withdrawing, but I refused to let it move me. I had long ago convinced myself I'd no real chance with her. I was only a friend and couldn't hope to be more, now less than ever if it turned out I was right.

"I'm sorry about your horses," she said as we moved down the slope to rejoin the others.

"What's done is done. I'll find some way to get them back, or the most of them. I'm pretty used to scrapin' the bottom of the barrel. Prospects are something I never really had, you know. I don't see much chance of hanging on to that spread."

She reached a hand to my arm and gave it a squeeze. "Begins to look like I'll not be able to keep mine, and you needn't bother saying if I'd stayed with cows I'd have a better chance." She said impulsively, "If it wasn't for you I guess I'd be about ready to give up."

I didn't know what to say to that, nor how she'd have felt if I'd shared this cockeyed notion. The kindness inherent in her nature, the impulsive way she could leap at things and go all out when it suited her whims made me certain I was right in saying no more than I had.

Hazel called, "You find anything up there?"

"Lot of ash and rock," I grumbled, swiveling a glance toward the setting sun. "Accordin' to my stomach it's time we were headin' for the nosebags."

And Terry said, "I hope those boys are back with our supplies."

They were back. "Have any trouble?" I asked Dude.

"Not to say trouble. We're back empty-handed. Store wouldn't give us no credit is all. Said from here on out it was cash on the barrel head."

Hiding my chagrin I said, "Go rope me a fresh bronc and I'll see what I can do. You stop in to see Reb?"

"Yeah—got a hook fitted onto him. Guess it's givin' him fits."

He came back with a fresh horse for me and two pack

animals. "I'll give you a blank check," Terry began, but I waved it away.

"Don't suppose my credit's any better'n yours, but I've still got enough in my jeans to buy grub—"

"At least wait till I've fixed you some supper," she urged.

"I'll get something in town," I said and, with the pack horses in tow, I rode out of the yard.

Dusk was already settling into night when I got onto the flats. There's a sort of luminous quality to nights in desert country that you'll find nowhere else. I'd no trouble seeing where I was going. I reckoned it behooved me to keep well away from Rock Springs and watchfully did so.

The store and saloons all showed they were open and Doc had a lamp in the window facing the street, which is where I went first. Lockhart gave me a sour look. Doc had the arm with no hand cradled in a sling, to keep him from bumping his handiwork probably. "How you doin', Reb?" I said. "You ready to go?"

The whole look of him changed. He surged out of his chair. "By Gawd, you know it!"

"Get your hook," I said, "and we'll be on our way." I paid his bill and helped him get strapped up after he took the arm out of its sling. We stopped at the livery and I bailed out his horse and saddled it for him and we rode to the store with our two pack horses.

I told the dour storekeeper, "Inman gave you a list of stuff for the Circle Dot. We've come to pick it up."

The man stared at Reb's hook then fetched his fish-eyed look back to me. "Let's see the color of your money, young feller. Any business I do with you hillbillies is strictly cash an' carry. Without you got the cash you don't carry."

"That's a good Christian attitude." I laid five twenties on

his counter. "Reckon them will take care of it?"

"Not quite. What do you want to leave off?"

I fished out a double eagle and plunked it down beside them and he went off to get up the stuff on Terry's list.

When he'd got it all assembled on the counter and I'd checked through it to be sure nothing essential was missing, I told him, "I'll need a couple burlaps."

"Be another two bucks."

I paid and he got them. When I got them packed the way I wanted I carried one outside to the nearest pack horse and lashed it onto the sawhorse saddle. Then I went back for the other and Reb, following me out, helped me anchor it on the other horse and we struck out for home.

Pulling into the yard I saw hitched before the house the slow fast horse I'd loaned Tolliver's man Mexico some ten or twelve days ago, when Tolliver had put six hundred sheep around the Bar B Cross headquarters. Without stopping to unpack or wait for Reb I took my spurs up onto the porch, yanked open the door and strode inside and saw the fellow in his cowhide vest, black hat pulled across the scar at his temple, sprawled in Terry's best chair like he owned the place.

I said through a tight throat, "What are you doin' here?"

"Just bein' neighborly. Thought I'd pay you a visit an' catch you up on the news."

I looked at Terry's blank face and the watchful expression in Hazel's half-shut stare. "What news?"

"Bein's we're on the same side in this here deal I figured you'd wanta know we've ate up all the graze around that place an' will prob'ly pull out in a day or two. Boss wants t' know if you'd like to borry a few hands."

"Yaquis?"

"Except for me that's all he'll use. Wants t' know too if he should burn the place down?"

I saw Terry shaking her head and said no. "We could use two maybe three hands if he can spare them. What's he aimin' to do for feed now?"

"Expect he'll be movin' onto Jolly's range. Kinda likes the notion of all them tanks."

I didn't much care for that grin on his face. I didn't care for him either with that two-fingered hand and his cocky self-assurance. In my book he'd all the earmarks of a first-class rogue. "I figure," he said, "with six hundred sheep we can prob'ly blanket every tank Jolly's got. When that happens you could buy him out cheap."

"Well," I said, "take care of yourself." I was turning to go and fetch in our supplies when that varmint said, "Elder's offered us your horses to get off his place."

CHAPTER
25

"Tolliver figuring to take them?"

"Why, bein's there's no feed left an' we got to move anyways, I expect he thinks that's a pretty good trade," he said, head cocked to one side to observe how I was taking it. "In his boots I reckon you'd think so too."

"He's got no bill of sale for those horses." I said flatly. "Anyone takes them off his hands will be guilty of receiving stolen goods."

Mexico laughed. "Claims the horses are his, that you been foreclosed, that the Bar B Cross has got a caretaker up there."

"That caretaker's dead," Hazel told him. "Dead and buried."

"We've retaken possession," I said, "and I'll take back those horses no matter who the hell's got them."

"Talk's cheap," said the irritating man. "Takes hard cash to buy good whiskey."

I was minded to cuff the miserable cur and had taken half a step to where I could reach him when he burst out again in that aggravating laugh. "Cool off," he snickered, "he's tryin' t' do you a favor an' take care of 'em for you till you've got a place to keep 'em."

Guess my jaw must have hung like a hoof-shaper's apron I was so taken aback.

And without more remarks he swaggered out of the house, got on the horse I had loaned him and tore off in a cloud of dust.

"You see what them bastards are up to, don't you?" Hazel burst out, looking thoroughly riled. "Eat up the range clear across them flats, a nice belt in the eye to every man in the cow business!"

"Sure," I said, seeing a lot more than that. "Then the sheep crowd, or Tolliver, will take over the country, buyin' those damn fools out for a song. Before they get on to what it's all about there won't be one cow left around here."

"Well," Terry said, "he's doing you a favor. You can't get around that."

"Sure he is," Lockhart said, stepping into the room with his hook in hand. "Looks like he wants you on his side."

And Hazel growled, "That son of a bitch don't think you're the mouse those cow boys have you pegged for."

"Nor do you!" declared Terry with a shine in her eyes that made me blink. "He's smart enough to know Gill's true worth—"

"And don't want him for an enemy," Reb Lockhart chipped in. "He's found out you'll fight." He chuckled with an approving look in my direction. "Same reason Mark threatened to close you out."

"Very flattering," I said dryly, "but it's a heap more likely it's Barbona he's not wanting against him—probably figures I've some kind of hold on that bandido. I suggest we put a little grub in our bellies."

So Terry went off to the kitchen to fix it.

Whatever it was that had moved Tolliver to favor me, I was more concerned right then with what I had discovered in that malapai. I wished now I had taken my luck in both hands and asked her to marry me before we had found it. To ask her . . . Hell, I almost wished we had never come onto it, because it would look like now if I opened my mouth I was after a rich wife and with no more scruples than that conniving Mark, out for all I could get.

I don't believe I really cared what others might say, but I would hate like anything for her to think that. What I had seen up there had just about made it impossible for me to speak, and I was so churned up by this view of the matter I was minded to find me a dog to kick.

CHAPTER
26

When she called us to supper and we'd all sat down I found it plumb awkward biting into my grub with two front choppers missing. Looked like I was going to have to get something done about it or have a heap of pleasure taken out of my eating. It was hard to believe two miserable teeth could make such a difference.

I got to thinking about Tolliver again. It was not hard to see what the fellow was up to. With a feud developing in this Four Corners country he'd been quick to figure where his best chance lay. With a squabble in the making between the Circle Dot and our bigger neighbors, the situation was ripe for him not only to pay off some long-standing grudge against the Bar B Cross but to drive the cow crowd clean off this range, and right now anyway it looked like he might do it. He was as far from being your run-of-the-mine sheepman as Piki Barbona, whom he'd called unpredictable.

He didn't want Barbona upsetting the apple cart. It cost him little to put me—and hence our tame bandit—on his side of the fence by taking care of my horses. The only drawback to this, far as I was concerned, was the overriding suspicion that when the time came he might refuse to give them up. I couldn't make myself believe that hard-nosed bugger's goodwill, once he got what he wanted, would last any longer than a June frost in the Mojave.

The only thing I could think of, if this suspicion proved well founded, was to work on Piki to help me get them back. I sure wasn't fool enough to think for a minute that cross-grained sheepman considered me any kind of match for himself. He'd have laughed at the notion I was tough enough to buck him. I know damn well I didn't think so, not without some mean-eyed help.

Piki came in as we were about to get up. Terry bade him pull up a chair. "I've kept something hot on the stove for you," she said and went off to fetch it.

Bill Hazel asked if he'd seen anything of interest. Barbona gave him that lopsided grin. "Seen a lot of sheep is all. Looks like Tolliver's gittin' ready to move."

Dude said we'd just been augurin' about it. "We figure he's fixin' to take over this whole range."

"Wouldn't surprise me," Piki agreed. "He's heard the owl hoot, that feller. A real *hombre malo* when he gits his back up. I remember three, four years ago he went into that cow country north of Vegas an' just about turned it upside down."

"What got him out of there?" Dude asked, curious.

"They brought in the soldiers, but he sure made it cost them."

"Them Paiutes take up for him?" Hazel wanted to know.

"Sure did. Whole damn tribe up an' went on the war-path."

"I don't think he can count on these Navajos helping," Terry said from the kitchen.

"Wouldn't bet on that," Hazel said. "They got sheep of their own and there's a passel of 'em ain't real happy where they're at."

After the talk broke off and most of them sought their

blankets, it occurred to me there might be something in what Hazel said. There were plenty of dissatisfied young bucks around who'd throw in with most anyone who promised some action and a few jugs of whiskey.

When I'd cleaned up my plate I quit the table and went outside with my rifle, wandering absentmindedly over to the corrals with night's darkness wrapped around me like a blanket. I had Terry in my head again.

You sort of take it for granted that after several months' acquaintance you've a pretty good notion what makes people click; what I mean is you generally figure you know the sort of person you're dealing with.

Come right down to it I didn't know her any more than she knew me. We'd no yardstick for really measuring each other. Impressions formed by another person's talk and actions are not necessarily accurate. There was much about Terry I couldn't even begin to know—the unspoken thoughts that shaped and moved her; I'd no way of guessing the sort of future she saw or wanted, or what she expected of it.

She'd had a rough time, brought up as she'd been to expect something a heap better than the loss of her father killed by a horse, her mother murdered right in front of her eyes; pursued by Mark and his brutal machinations, and now my sudden discovery. Whatever these things had done to the real her I'd no means of knowing. Shock on shock could change nearly anyone.

I didn't think she was bitter, but couldn't believe she regarded me with the degree of wanting I had for her. Why the hell would she? I was the orphan brought up by Mark's father; a devious-minded galoot of poor prospects, if indeed I now had any at all, only moderately ambitious with damn little right now I could call my own.

I tongued the gap in my teeth I had got from Mark's

knee and tried to think what to do about my horses without laying hold of any satisfying notions. I reckoned I'd just have to wait and see. I was still out there among the night's darker shadows when I saw Piki outlined against the lamplit window and realized with a start he was out of the house and catfooting toward me.

I dropped a hand to the gun that swung at my hip, watching him narrow the space between us, remembering Tolliver's remarks about this fellow. Unpredictable, the sheepman had called him; certainly his pair of Yaquis still on our payroll were—to my way of thinking—no more reliable than a woman's watch. Loyal they might be— even Piki too—but their goodwill was nothing a fellow could bank on.

It was said of Barbona he could see in the dark. The abrupt hunch of his shape against the house lights and that soft snorting laugh was obvious assurance he knew where my hand was and what it had hold of.

"Yes?" I said, not relinquishing my grip.

Barbona's laugh was this time full throated. But whatever he'd intended was suddenly forgotten as the lifting pound of onrushing hoofs stiffened both of us.

Straight into the yard that rider came, and against the house lights made a gravel-spurting stop just this side of the porch. "Edwardo!" I called on an outrush of breath as we both sprinted toward him. "What's up?"

"The sheep—the cow boys," he cried, "are driving them toward the cliff!"

Now everyone in the house was out and Barbona's two Yaquis came up on the run. "Let's go!" Piki yelled and we dived for our saddles. In less than two minutes every man in our outfit was flogging his horse in the direction of the trouble.

The moon creeping over those distant crags began to light

up our way as we drove full tilt through the grays and blacks of that rugged terrain, grim-faced with worry, all of us knowing what the loss of those sheep would mean to Terry.

Going as direct as the ground would allow, it was no great while before we had them in sight, that dark grayish blur of the panicked animals pursued by the racket of yelling horsebackers, ourselves never noticed in that bedlam of noise. There were no dogs to head them or turn them aside, and with the cliff no more than a mile away, Edwardo with swinging quirt and flashing spurs was doing his damndest to get up there and turn them as Piki's Yaquis opened up with their Winchesters.

One of those dark shapes was knocked from his saddle and two horses went down as we closed the gap, and Lockhart's rebel yell sailed through the turmoil as the blast of his shotgun blew a hole through the uproar. Now, sheep forgotten, Mark's bunch were returning our fire, and it was like we were riding through a swarm of hornets.

It had seemed to me when I'd first caught sight of them there had been eight riders harrying our sheep; now there appeared to be no more than five, which was what I thought we had with our Navajo trying to get ahead of the sheep. But it was plain the Bar B Cross had not been looking for any interference; our unexpected arrival had badly disconcerted them, and two of their number were a deal more interested in preserving their health than engaging in any showdown fight.

The remaining three, with a last burst of firing, took off hell-for-leather to get themselves out of the way of our bullets. But just as they probably figured to have achieved this one of our Yaquis knocked another off his horse.

"Come on!" Barbona shouted, "let's git the rest of 'em!"

"Never mind them," Terry yelled, fiercely angry. "It's a sight more important to save those sheep!"

CHAPTER
27

It was the first I'd known that Terry had been with us. Piki Barbona cried in a passion, "We'll never git a better chance at them vandals!" But she had her way and the rest of us galloped off after Edwardo and only just managed to get the woollies turned in time to keep them from joining the ones Ace Jolly had destroyed.

When we came to take stock it was plain that damned bandit had ignored her orders and gone after Mark's crowd. "Serve him right if they gang up and kill him," Bill Hazel declared with a snort of disgust.

I didn't reckon they would. He'd a lot more experience than that bunch could boast of. We'd just got the flock back to their previous location when Barbona came riding up on his lathered horse. Terry berated him and Piki gave her that lopsided grin, but had the good sense to keep his mouth shut.

We left his two Yaquis with Edwardo to keep an eye on the sheep and headed for home. We came across a pair of Piki's shot dogs, two dead Bar B Cross horses and one of Mark's crew, also dead. No sign of any others, but Dude opined there'd be at least two others nursing wounds for a while, which I was inclined to think might well leave Mark shorthanded for a spell without he could hire some replacements. I didn't think under the circumstances he'd be finding that easy.

Still probing the gap left by two missing teeth, I decided to ride to town and see if I could get something done about it. Terry tried to get me to put it off, but when I insisted she sent Piki with me.

After we'd got clear of the others I asked him what he'd found out and he said Tolliver's sheep were all over Jolly's range. He said, "I reckon you hit the nail on the head. Sure looks like he's got it in mind to do what Elder was up to an' take over this country. All of it anyway that's west of these hills."

I didn't reckon we could count Mark out of this. He might have to go a ways to build up his crew again, but he had plenty of money and the Bar B Cross was the sort of big outfit hired guns liked to work for. An outfit with clout. I felt sure in my own mind we'd not seen the last of him. Nothing but death was going to keep him from grabbing onto that land.

Four Corners didn't have but one dentist. The fellow worked from his house on the far edge of town; we had to go right through the main drag to get there, which might be safer at night, but I was keeping my eyes peeled. It was while we were walking our horses past the Ajax Saloon that I heard Mark's hectoring voice.

Barbona had his Winchester laid across his lap and my own right hand was on the butt of my pistol till we'd reached our destination. "No lights," Barbona grunted. "Gone to bed like as not."

"Take our horses out back while I get him up."

"Was I you I'd be makin' far apart tracks."

"Go ahead an' make 'em if that's how you see it."

I got off my horse, went up and pounded on the door. Piki grabbed up their reins and went off with both horses toward the back of the house. I pounded some more. About the time I was ready to use the butt of my six-shooter the door was jerked open by a long-nosed galoot in a nightcap who looked mad enough to chew barbed wire. "I don't work at night. If you got somethin' ailin' you come back tomorrow—"

"Keep your voice down," I growled with a fistful of nightgown, hauling him close. "I've come a far piece an' ain't minded to wait." He had a lamp in one hand, and I backed him inside with the snout of my pistol prodding his belly. "You see where those teeth were? I want 'em replaced."

In a surly tone he wanted to know if I'd fetched the teeth.

"I'm goin' to fetch you something if you don't get busy!"

Barbona edged in and shut the door. "He gonna fix 'em or ain't he?"

"He'll fix them," I said and put up my gun. "Man'll do anything to stay out of boot hill."

He backed off a piece and set down his lamp. "Wait till I get some clothes on."

"Fixing my face don't require no clothes. Come on. Let's get at it."

He backed into another room, us following, Piki bringing the lamp. "Two pegged teeth," this tooth-mauler said, "will cost you—"

"What do you mean 'pegged'?"

"They'll have to be screwed into your jaw."

While I was wrestling with second thoughts, Barbona said, "You do this right you got nothin' to worry about."

"I better give him some laudanum. Screwin' two teeth in won't be no picnic—"

"No laudanum," I told him, not minded to find myself put to sleep.

He said, looking nervous, "I'm goin' to have to dig out those roots, and if you don't sit still—"

"Just get on with it," I said, and climbed into the chair.

He took the lamp from Piki and set it on a shelf a foot away from my head, then he lit a second lamp and placed it beside it. "Open your mouth."

That has to have been the most miserable hour I had ever put in. Bar none.

When he held up a mirror for me to admire his handiwork I was of two minds whether to look or not; but except for the smears of blood I reckoned I seemed pretty much as I always had. I managed a nod and, dampening the bib he'd put over my shirtfront, he cleaned off my face. "Fifty bucks that'll be, and I'm lettin' you off cheap."

Despite that being very near the wages from two months work for an average cowhand, I was too worn down to argue about it, though it mighty near cleaned me out of ready cash.

Barbona said, "You wait here till I git the horses."

"Pain'll wear off in a week or two most likely," I was assured by the doc through a pleased sort of grin. "Feel free to come back anytime," he added as I got unsteadily out of his chair.

"Never mind the lamp," I grunted and, feeling my way down the hall, pulled open the door soon as the hoof sound stopped in front of it. Piki said as I got into the saddle, "How's it feel?"

"Feels like I been kicked in the face by a mule," I growled with several choice epithets.

"This may git a mite sticky," Barbona informed me. "I been lookin' around. Mark Elder's in town with a pair of his understrappers. Might be we could avoid 'em if—"

"Go ahead," I said nastily, "if you're scared to face up to them," and turned my horse to go back through town the same way I'd come into it. It was probably the pain that was flogging up my temper; I wasn't the kind that was usually that stupid.

Barbona pulled the rifle out from under his leg and laid it across his pommel. Close as our mounts would let him get he muttered, "I think there's one of 'em hunkered alongside the store. Where the others is at I got no idea, but I'll take care of him. When I yell *go* you pile on the timber."

All of a sudden I didn't feel so rambunctious. There was sweat on the hand that gripped my colt as with narrowed stare I probed the roundabout deeper patches of black, turning up nothing that increased my alarm. I didn't think we'd been spotted on our way in and looked again at the store corner without discovering anyone. With anyone but Piki I'd have assumed he'd imagined it.

Abruptly swinging his Winchester storeward, he yelled "Go!" and triggered twice as, crouched along his neck, I raked my horse into a headlong run. With a bloodcurdling yell Barbona loosed another shot just as muzzle-flame spat from the deep black alongside the store.

As I barreled past another gun flashed from the saloon's swinging doors and I drove a couple slugs that way without discernible result. Piki fired again as we left town behind and back there someplace somebody yelled.

CHAPTER
28

"Damn poor shootin' all around," Piki growled.

Personally I was glad to have escaped intact. I said, "That last shot of yours must've got somebody."

"Nicked him is all," Barbona said, disgusted. "I should have clobbered that one by the store. Where we headed for?"

"Home, I reckon. I'm not in much case for swappin' lead right now."

He said after a moment, "If I did more than nick that feller—if, I mean, it keeps him off a horse, the Bar B Cross should be runnin' short of hands. By my count, anyhow, he ain't got but three hands in fightin' shape."

"Someone said a while back he didn't have but six. He lost at least one going after Terry's sheep. I figure at least two more were hit, countin' that one just now, he may not have more than two."

"There's always third-rate guns hangin' round the saloons. No trouble for Elder to pick up some of them. May have done so already."

By the time we reached the Circle Dot the sun was peering over the hills behind us and I caught the good smell of

Arbuckle's coffee, and it came over me that all-gone feeling I'd had rumbling through my gizzard was mostly kicked up by hunger.

There was a strange horse tethered to one of the porch posts and Piki said as we got out of our saddles, "Villalobos," and a sound of voices drifted out of the house.

Gun in hand, Bill Hazel was half out of his chair as we came through the door. With a sheepish grin he let go of the gun when he saw who it was; and I saw Diego Quintares installed in Terry's best chair. "Been talking politics," Reb Lockhart said after we'd done with greetings and I had shaken the Don's hand. Dude wanted to know if I'd got mumps so I flashed my new teeth at him. I guessed we should've cuffed the dust off our clothes but my face hurt so bad I hadn't thought to do it.

Terry, hustling off to the kitchen, said over her shoulder we should get ourselves some coffee while she fried up some eggs and bacon and heated us up some chopped turnip greens. "The rest of us," she said, "have already eaten," and asked Quintares if he'd have another cup. He said he would and Barbona went after her to fetch it in. With my jaw like it was I didn't reckon to get much down.

The subject of Tolliver's sheep came up and apparently they'd already talked some about it, because Quintares wanted to know if I thought they meant to come through these hills, and I said I didn't believe so. "He's got his eye on those flats, and now that Mark Elder's run off those two-bit owners I expect Tolliver aims to take over that whole valley if he can."

"If you're worried about your place I'll be glad to loan you half a dozen *váqueros.*"

I explained about Mark having seized my horses and traded them to Tolliver to get him off the Bar B Cross. And how Tolliver had sent me word he'd take care of them for me till I had a place to put them. "If he shouldn't want to give them up when I'm ready, I'd be glad for the loan of some of your hands," I said, and he nodded.

Terry called us to eat and I followed Piki into the kitchen with my cup, which she filled again for me. I hoped Barbona would have sense enough not to mention we'd run into trouble on our way out of town; I was feeling real protective toward Terry just then and reckoned it would only get her upset again. The sheriff's name was mentioned disparagingly and Dude Inman opined the fellow was showing great political savvy in staying completely away from this fracas.

"While people are being killed right and left!" our Irish owner called from the kitchen. "I think he ought to be tarred and feathered!"

"You bet." Our bandit made haste to show which side of the fence he was on.

And Terry, putting her head through the door, wanted to know what were the qualifications most necessary if a person wanted to run for the office, and Reb Lockhart said, "He'd have to be alive."

After the laughs and grins and catcalls Terry said, coming into the room, "I'm asking for information, boys."

I said, "You're not hankerin' for that job, are you?"

"Yes I am," she declared, defiant. "Is there anything to keep a woman from being sheriff?"

"Anyone can run," Hazel answered, "if he can get his party's nomination."

"And how do you go about doing that?"

Don Diego Quintares, rasping a hand along his jaw with a thoughtful look, said, "I'll see that you're nominated if you'll stand for the office."

I was too startled to open my mouth. I guess the rest were in the same boat. In the sudden quiet Terry said with her chin up, "It will be my pleasure. I believe the law should be fair to all parties and administered impartially."

"Hear, hear!" cried the irrepressible Piki Barbona.

"When you're ready to go in and file," Quintares said to her, "I'll see that you have an impressive escort, enough of a one to make certain you get there."

"There's only two days to the deadline for filing," Dude pointed out.

"We'll pick you up here tomorrow." Quintares nodded. "Eight o'clock suit you?"

Over at the bunkhouse after the Villalobos owner had taken his departure there emerged two schools of thought about the idea of Terry running for sheriff. The predominant belief held that a woman's place was in the home, occupying herself with the rearing of future citizens. That she couldn't be elected anyway, for what man would be fool enough to vote for a woman?

"Well," Dude Inman said with a grin, "I would if she's pretty as Terry."

And Bill Hazel, nodding, seriously allowed, "I think a lot of fellers would."

"Be stickin' her neck out," Lockhart growled. "I don't think we should let her do it."

"Take a pretty stout hand to molest a female," Piki objected.

"Mark Elder already has," Hazel said grimly, "an' gotten away with it."

I couldn't decide how I would feel about having folks hang a star on her chest; it was in my mind, along with Bill Hazel, it might very well happen if for no other reason than that she *was* a woman. The scalawags and scoundrels would be all for it. So would the great bulk of the cowboys and a lot of townfolks that were fed up with the sheriff we already had.

More and more I was being led to the conclusion there would be no comfort or peace in this country so long as Mark was free to perpetrate his villainies. Inescapably I had begun to believe that nothing but his death could put an end to the killings and horrors we all seemed to be caught up in. Mark Elder's death looked like the only solution.

And having gone this far through the twists of my thinking, against my will I was becoming convinced that sooner or later, unless something intervened, I was like to become the instrument of his destruction.

Yet I could not see myself killing Mark. He ought right now to be behind bars, no two ways about it. He had treated me abominably . . . likewise Terry . . . killing Terry's mother who had been all for him . . . deliberately smashing Reb's hand and all.

Occasionally I had grimly wondered if my being chained all that day in the blast of the sun wasn't back of my feeling Mark would have to be killed.

I did not want to think so. But it was plain as paint something was going to have to be done. Regardless of what Tolliver and his sheep succeeded in doing to this Four Corners range, nothing but his death was going to keep Mark away from grabbing this ranch, not if he'd seen what I had on that hogback and come as he must have to a similar conclusion.

CHAPTER
29

True to his word Quintares rode into the yard next morning with a full dozen of his vaqueros to accompany Terry to the county seat. It had been decided beforehand between Terry and me that the rest of us should remain at the Circle Dot to hold the fort against all and any comers. This place, I felt sure, was Mark's prime concern; and despite Tolliver's apparent goodwill I imagined him quite capable of mingling our sheep right in with his own. Even using them to spearhead his drive.

"How long," I asked Quintares, "do you reckon to be gone?"

"We should be back here again sometime tomorrow night."

Terry came out and mounted the horse Hazel had caught up and saddled for her, and scarcely longer than it takes to tell they were all on their way to toss her hat in the ring.

It occurred to me that Tolliver, when the time came, would take advantage of the election drawing people to the polls to consolidate his gains and make himself master of every bit of valley range not under the Bar B Cross iron. And I considered it not unlikely he might even preempt that.

And Mark, counting on us all going in to vote for Terry, would—if he could pick up more hands—be figuring to take over the Circle Dot. For it wasn't at all likely he'd believe she could be elected.

Reb Lockhart, as her oldest hand, had been left in charge and straightaway sent one of Piki's two remaining Yaquis up onto that high point back of the house to keep a sharp watch for any sign of trouble.

He then suggested the rest of us should have some kind of strategy session and, hopefully, arrive at some means for spiking Mark's guns, when and if.

With jaw and face still giving me considerable misery I doubted I'd have much to contribute but sat in anyway. Piki Barbona in his usual flamboyant style declared what we ought to do in this dog-eat-dog situation was hunt Mark down and make an end of him, stringing up any of his outfit we were able to come on to.

Lockhart, wearing his hook, was all for this and made no bones about saying so, decorating his vote with some choice bits of blasphemy. Dude was undecided but Hazel was against it. "We don't know where he's at. If we go chasing around trying to find him we'll be giving him a chance to do the very thing we're hoping to prevent."

"What's that?" asked the only Yaqui invited to this pow-wow.

"Taking over this place while we're off on a goose chase," Bill Hazel grumbled. "Even if he's given up his grassless headquarters in a trade for Gill's horses, I doubt that we'll find him there."

"Who do you suppose is keepin' an eye on his cows?" Reb asked.

They all looked at me. I passed, but Bill Hazel said, "You ought to know him better than anyone."

"All right," I said. "I doubt if he's even thinking about

cows right now. Way it looks to me . . . grabbin' the Circle Dot, and hanging on to it once he moves in, just about has to be his first consideration. I'll give odds he's scoutin' this place right now."

"Or has someone doin' it for him," Dude said. "I vote we stay right where we're at." Which is what we finally decided to do.

Dude Inman in his fancified clothes and pearl-gray beaver elected to get up on the high ground with Piki's number-one Yaqui and, rifle in hand, departed. Lockhart, temporary boss of this outfit with a sawed-off Greener held by the barrel across his left shoulder, beckoned me aside to growl, "I've got no more idea what to do now than a confounded gopher! You got any notions?"

"Maybe you ought to send Piki's other Yaqui off to help Edwardo keep an eye on the sheep, just in case."

"Thought it was your notion—"

The rest of whatever Lockhart had been about to say was cut off by Dude's shout from above: "Hey! Somebody's cut that Yaqui's throat!"

I guess all four of us there in the yard stared like fools toward the sound of Dude's voice. Barbona swore. Lockhart ran scrambling up the hill to see for himself and Bill Hazel, peering at me, angrily asked, "How could anyone git up to that feller without us seein' him?"

"Reckon," I said, "we'll likely never know, but the way Reb's going ain't the only way up there. Every hill's got four sides an' we've got hills all around us. Looks like Mark's changed his tactics."

When Hazel stood staring, I said, "I'm off to see if they've picked off Edwardo; rest of you better stay in sight of each other."

Without hanging round to discuss the thing further I

roped out a horse and headed for Terry's sheep. If, instead
of direct confrontation, Mark was resorting to picking us
off one by one, there wasn't much we could do but what
I'd just said—keep in sight of each other. This would limit
our choices and give him the edge. If what I thought was
the answer to what he was up to—as I was sure it was—
this new tactic would just about immobilize us, not only
compelling us to stay together but marooning us here to
prevent him taking over the spread.

Another notion this fetched into my head was what this
could do to our nerves and tempers. A further worry wrapped
itself round my gut in the remembrance of my failed attempt
to take Mark prisoner. If he could manage to grab Terry he
would win hands down, forcing us to accept any terms he
was minded to make.

With these thoughts for company, topping a brushy knoll
I saw Terry's sheep scattered in little browsing clumps all
across half a mile of tawny ground and no horseman in
sight. No horse in sight either.

It took the better part of twenty minutes to find Edwardo,
shot through the back and gone, I hoped, to a better place.

Having nothing to dig with and not stout enough to climb
back on my horse with him in my arms I left him there for
the buzzards and coyotes, a loyal hand who'd deserved a
better fate.

It was crowding noon when I rode into the yard and told
what I'd found. Reb Lockhart swore. The rest with tight
faces didn't say anything. It wasn't hard to guess what they
were thinking. Two down, four to go. Hazel finally said,
"We better eat," and started for the house.

Calling after him I said, "I'll take soup if you want to fix
it," remembering the bacon and eggs I'd swallowed damn
near whole.

"Better fix it yourself if you don't want to settle for refried beans."

I told him, scowling, I'd take the beans, and dropped a hip on the porch rail out of the sun. Barbona, anchoring burly shoulders against a wall, declared frijoles to be his favorite fruit. Nobody laughed or felt like grinning.

When it was ready, warmed up from the night before, we picked up tin plates, took as much as we wanted and sat down at the table. Even this gooey muck in my present condition was hard to get down. About the only thing I could comfortably manage was reheated java from the pot on the stove.

"What do we do now?" Reb asked through a mouthful. For a southpaw forced by that hook to do everything right-handed he was making out pretty well, a deal better than I'd expected. Made me feel like a chump asking for soft grub on account of two teeth screwed into my jaw. Reb had perked up considerable since getting away from that sawbones.

I was about to air once again my conviction that what Mark was after was the Circle Dot when a rush of hoof sound brought us out of our chairs in a dash for the door. "Looks like one of Quintares' vaqueros," Hazel said bodingly as we erupted onto the planks of the porch. In his chin-strapped sombrero and tight-fitting pants he certainly looked like one of the dozen who had gone off with Terry, and the hurried way he came into the yard pulling up in a cloud of dust turned my mouth dry and stuck the breath in my throat.

"Name's Chico," he called as he got off his horse with a flash of big-rowelled spurs. "Don Diego sent me back to say they might be delayed. Office was closed and locked up when we got there. Sign on the door said nine A.M. to four P.M., so they had to stay over—thought you might think they'd run into trouble."

"See to his horse, Bill," Lockhart said and, to Chico, he said, "we got beans on the stove—come in an' eat a bite."

"Gracias," the man said, and followed Reb into the house looking pleased.

I went along with Hazel as he led the fellow's horse toward the day pen. Catching the slanchways stare he sent in my direction, I said, "Reckon you got the same notion I did, seein' that ranny comin' hell for hootin'."

"Yeah. Thought mebbe they'd been ambushed."

"Ought to've known better. Take a sizable outfit to tie into that many."

"Pretty hard-lookin' geezer," Hazel noted. "Wouldn't be a bad thing if we could keep him here awhile. Don't know about you, but what happened to that Yaqui an' your Navajo on top of it has me reachin' for my iron ever' time somethin' moves."

We took off his gear and put the horse behind bars with a chunk of alfalfa. Both corrals had water piped from the house, one of the improvements Terry's dad had put in. Hazel said, "Might help your jaw if you'd swish some salt water around them teeth four or five times a day while we're here."

"We ought to have somebody up on that point," I said, tipping my head back to sweep a look over it. "How about putting Quintares' man up there?"

"All right with me, but it's Reb you better check with. He's feelin' his oats a bit, playin' top dog while the boss is away."

When he crossed the yard with me walking alongside and came up to where the rest of the outfit was taking their unaccustomed ease on the porch, it appeared that Reb had already picked Dude Inman for that chore, and our Fancy

Dan didn't look at all overjoyed with the prospect. He was muttering under his breath as he passed us on his way to tackle the climb.

"Sooner him than me," Bill Hazel said and grinned.

We sat down on the steps. I had picked up a stick to whittle on and was getting out my knife when the new man, belching, came out of the kitchen to lounge against the rail. "Have much settin' around at your place?" asked Piki.

"Quintares don't hold with settin' around. Good man to work for though," the fellow admitted. "Feeds well and puts on a chicken-pull every third week. Man can get along fine long's he looks like bein' busy."

I said, "Must tax your ingenuity," and Chico grinned. "Always leather to soap, harness to mend, a horse to rub down or a post to straighten. We've all become experts," he said with a chuckle.

We sat around within call, waiting I suppose for something to happen. About the middle of the afternoon Reb, getting up, allowed it was time to send up a fresh lookout. "We had a man killed up there this mornin'," he said to Chico. "You want to take a whack at it?"

Chico stared. "The señor makes joke—no?"

"No," Reb said. "They say lightnin' never strikes in the same place but once. But of course," he mentioned, smiling down at the man, "if you don't care to risk it I'll send Gill."

And Barbona, the irrepressible, said, "I'd as soon be up in that windy open as hunkerin' here where the blue whistlers fly."

Chico, eyeing him distastefully, turned back to Lockhart. "Killed how?"

"Some rannihan handy with a knife," Piki said, "cut his throat."

Quintares' man looked from one to the other of us as

though suspecting his leg was being pulled. "I'll go," I growled and picked up my rifle.

Chico said as if the whole conversation offended him, "We'll both of us go," and Lockhart handed him a Winchester.

We'd had horses up there a couple of times but this wasn't any climb a man would tackle for the hell of it. What with loose rock and slides you had to watch your step and Chico, a short bull of a man, brushing Barbona out of his way, took off in the lead like he was minded to keep it. But I was right on his heels and not once was the cocky five-footer ever out of my sight.

With the rim a scant two feet over my hat the fellow, topping out, on a hoarse indrawn breath cried, *"Madre de Dios!"* stopping so short I went barging into him. Throat constricting, fighting off nausea, I saw what had turned Quintares' man taut.

Crumpled up almost under his feet was the lookout we'd come up to replace.

CHAPTER
30

Dead as a doornail.

The gut-clutching horror of it left me speechless.

Staring at the blood welling out of him, one awful fact got through to me straightoff: Unlike the Yaqui we had found this morning, this second one had been alive only moments ago, yet we'd neither of us heard so much as a gasp.

"Knifed!" Chico muttered. There was no doubt of that with the haft sticking out of his chest in plain sight. Stepping round him with the breath hung up in my throat, I knew we ought to search for the assassin but was still too shocked to get any words out. It was Chico who called down to the others, as cool by God as though discovering cadavers was an everyday occurrence.

Scrambling up onto the rim, Barnona snarled, "Son of a bitch!" furious at the loss of the last of his Indians. Eyes flashing round like he figured to jerk the culprit out of thin air, he went crashing off into the brush with great strides, myself on his heels and Dude Inman behind me. Hazel took off in a different direction and Lockhart and Chico in yet another. None of us until too late thought of looking for sign, and by that time you couldn't tell one track from any other that made sense.

We spent an hour in this fashion before we gave up.

With the rest of us going back down to the house, each battling hard thoughts, Barbona and Inman stayed up there, covering him with stones to keep off the predators, grim with orders to remain as lookouts.

Hazel cooked up some grub that left much to be desired stacked up against the flavorsome meals we'd been getting from Terry.

I don't guess anyone did much sleeping but the night finally passed without further alarms. With dawn rolling over the roundabout hills Lockhart sent me and Hazel up to relieve our sentinels and allow them a chance to put some food in their bellies.

Three men dead by the hand of that killer was the thought I took up there, and nothing to show who or where the bugger was. "Gives a feller the willies just thinkin' about it," Hazel growled. "I would sure like to git my hands on that jasper."

"We been acing pretty stupid havin' only one man up here as lookout."

"That cat-footed killer won't be findin' us so easy."

I thought that was something to hope for.

A couple hours later Chico came up to take my place, saying the segundo wanted me down at the house.

"What's up?" I said as Reb came to meet me in the middle of the yard.

"Don't know as anything is," Lockhart grumbled, "just thought I'd feel better with you down here."

That sent my brows up. "You mean safer?" I said, considerably astonished. "I'd have reckoned Chico or Hazel was more your kind of hombre. I'm no pistolero."

"I know that," Reb said and frowned, "but you're a feller

that uses his head for somethin' besides a hatrack. You reckon we'll ever catch up with that killer?"

"Expect if he keeps usin' that knife one of us may get lucky. You got any table salt?"

"What d'you want that for?"

"My jaw," I said, and went into the kitchen hunting it, half expecting that knifer to spring out of some corner. I knew it was silly, but we hadn't lost him up there by more than short moments. If we'd only thought to look for his tracks we might have got him by now—I mean, looked for them soon as we'd found that dead Yaqui.

Guess I still had a chip on my shoulder on account of Hazel likening me to a mouse a few days ago; there couldn't be anybody that liked that kind of comparison. It wasn't that I was scared of getting hurt. I was aggressive enough in my own mind; it was just that I liked to take a good look before I leaped into anything I could later be sorry for. I'd always been the quiet sort, even as a kid. Just show me that killer and folks would find out!

It bothered me some considerable to think Terry may have got the same notion as Hazel. Maybe I just wasn't pushy enough, too shy for my own good was the way some might look at it. "Gill," I told myself, "you better get out of that rut and get whacking." In times like these in this kind of country it was the squeaky wheel that got the most grease.

It was drawing on to late evening again with the shadows stretching out longer and blacker with a hot wind blowing in off the desert, when we channeled our way through the troughs between hills. I could hear the leaves twittering high up in the cottonwoods and was impatient with waiting for Terry to get back. If it ever got into Mark's head to grab her, as I'd tried to nab him and he had nabbed me, he would have us between a rock and a hard place, just about able to dictate his own terms.

I sure as hell wished that thought hadn't hit me. Hazel had just fed the horses in the day pen when Reb called us in to swill down some supper. "No use waitin' for Terry, I guess—accordin' to Chico it'll prob'ly be mornin' before they show up."

"Where is the little bounder?" Hazel wanted to know.

Barbona said, "Gone back on top. Said he would stand the first trick by himself."

"That waddy," Hazel grunted, "is rougher than a cob. If the rest of Quintares' hands is like him I'm not surprised Mark Elder ain't botherin' Villalobos."

"We don't know that he ain't," I heard myself saying. "Taking a dozen vaqueros just to make sure Terry gets a chance to throw her hat in the ring seems to me rather much, now I've had time to think about it."

The whole push turned their heads to have a look at me. Following my new resolution, I said, "Supposing Mark has hatched up a deal with Quintares. . . ."

"What kinda deal?" Dude Inman asked, hitching forward in his chair.

"To take Terry O'Brian out of circulation."

The place got so quiet I could hear my heart thump.

CHAPTER
31

Bill Hazel said, "You ain't serious are you?"

All of them hanging on my words, I said, "Look at it this way. On the face of things, Villalobos—if you set out to grab anything—would have to be the choicest plum. But Quintares can call up more men than all the rest of these outfits put together—no use battin' your head against a wall, man smart as Mark would figure how to get some good out of it."

Appearing more than half sold already, Lockhart wanted to know what good.

"If we accept as fact Mark's primary aim is to grab the Circle Dot," I said, "a logical first step should be to lay hold of the owner. But until that owner comes to terms, the next thing wanted more than anything else is a safe-keeping place that, even if suspected, can't be breached. Villalobos fits all the requirements."

That seemed so likely it almost sold *me*. Having made the desired impression I couldn't think now what to do with it. This was no time to flounder. Unexpectedly Dude Inman came along with what he figured to be help. "That's right," he said. "With Quintares' rep nobody'd suspect him of bein' involved—bet she never got near the county seat!"

Barbona yelled, "What're we waitin' on?"

In the shine from the lamps what I could see of the windows back of Terry's lace curtains was now solid black. Seeing their faces as they snatched up rifles heading for the door, I stared in dismay at the mountain I'd built from a molehill and thought of the avalanche about to get loose. All I'd been up to was to get some attention, which just goes to show—But don't ask me what.

Before I was able to undo this mischief we could all hear the sound of approaching horses, and as we rushed outside they pulled up in the yard and Terry's voice called, "What's the commotion? Is everything all right?"

Her three hands and Barbona were all staring at me, and now that it had happened I didn't care at all to be the center of attention and hustled to get my oar in before some fool blurted out the big windy I'd concocted. Some truth looked called for, and in a skreaky sort of voice I said, "There's a killer loose round here someplace, got both of Piki's Yaquis and that Navajo kid I had watchin' your sheep."

With Terry looking her dismay, through the tinkle of rowels and creaking saddle leather Quintares gave a sharp order in Spanish, and with his crew beginning to spread out as though to beat the brush it came suddenly over me that all twelve of them were aboard their horses right here in the yard. "Wait!" I called, throwing up a hand. "Did or didn't you," I said to their boss, "send a rider to tell us that office was closed and you'd be late getting back?"

"Of course not," Quintares said, puzzled. "The office was open."

With a startled oath Barbona was off at a run, Hazel and Inman hard on his heels, all three of them headed for the high ground back of the house, the lookout point where both Yaquis had been killed, hustling to get their hands on Chico.

• • •

Feeling a bigger chump than I'd looked in the first place I explained about Chico. "But how," Terry asked, "with you right behind him, could this fellow possibly have killed that Yaqui without you knowing it?"

"I don't know," I grumbled, "but he must have done it."

"Where could he have come from?" Quintares asked.

"I don't know that either," I said, more willing to look a fool than stick my neck out again. "How did things go at the county seat?"

"Well," Terry answered, "I filed—for whatever that's worth. Those people up there tried to talk me out of it, said I'd never be elected."

"You may be surprised," Don Diego said and smiled. "Not everyone's happy with the present incumbent."

Terry invited them all in to eat, but Quintares said no, they'd better be getting home, and Barbona shouted down from above they'd found nobody up there.

By the time the three of them rejoined us the Villalobos contingent had departed and Lockhart had gone in to stir up something for Terry to eat.

"Well," Hazel said, "you pretty near had me convinced. You made a good case but I'm glad you were wrong."

"Yes, well, I was wrong about Quintares," I freely admitted, "but the rest of it's sound if Mark happens to think of it. He might even take a chance on grabbin' her himself. We'd better keep our eyes peeled."

"How do you figure Chico?" Barbona wanted to know.

"I can't think why I didn't catch him at it, bein' right behind him, but he must be the one that's been killin' them."

"My notion, too," Dude told us. "Feller's almost sure to be working for Mark. Be open season on that jigger if I ever get him lined up in my sights."

I guess we all felt the same about that. "Be a case," I said, "of shoot an' talk later. Bound to know he'll get no chance at the rest of us. Did you look for tracks?"

"I looked," Hazel said, "but the breeze kept blowin' my matches out; too many tracks to pick out his sign. I'm not bettin' he'll not try again. He's pretty handy with a knife; he didn't have time to retrieve it this last job, but I'd give odds he's got another tucked away on him someplace."

"That's a real happy thought," Dude Inman said, scowling. "Goin' to fix me up with a nice set of dreams."

CHAPTER
32

When Barbona's idea of hunting Mark down had first come up I'd seen several objections, principal of which was that while we were scouring around trying to find him we'd be handing him a first-class chance to move in and take over. I'd give pretty long odds he was keeping cases on us. But instead of hanging round waiting to be picked off by his killer, if only one of us camped on his trail, leaving the rest to guard Terry and the ranch, the notion might have some merit.

As long as he was loose to implement his schemes we were not going to have much peace around here and, right or wrong, it was in my head it was going to be me that would have to take care of him. This posed some problems. I thought of wrapping a derringer up in my fist, but reluctantly discarded this. If it came to a shoot-out between us and I was the lucky survivor, it would have to be seen as self-defense or I would damn sure hang.

First thing after breakfast next morning Terry got hold of me to say there'd be nobody else spending the night on that point. Nobody. "Unless there's a moon, having someone up there doesn't make any sense. There've been more than enough deaths on the Circle Dot already."

There had to be some solution to the fix we were in other than turning over the ranch to that cross-grained son of my former benefactor. But the only solution that came to mind required meeting Mark across the sights of a six-shooter, and from whichever angle I chose to survey this it seemed always to be me that got fitted for the coffin.

Terry, it appeared, had gone right on talking, but I was jerked to attention when she said rather tartly, "You haven't heard a thing I've said!"

"I know it," I admitted. "I've been trying to find us some way out of this." She probably saw from my tone I hadn't succeeded.

She said, trying out a reluctant notion, "Perhaps if I turned over—"

"Don't say it," I growled. "If worse comes to worst I could probably dry-gulch him."

"And if push comes to shove, I—"

"Well, you couldn't," I said, "because I wouldn't let you."

She peered at me, startled. "Sometimes I would swear I don't know you at all."

We stared at each other trying to read what was back of faces grown too familiar and making, on my part anyway, a damn poor job of it. At last I shrugged and she said, "If I could know what's back of this change in Mark, if I could understand what's driving him—"

"Wouldn't make any difference if you did."

"Has he lost his marbles?"

"I don't think so. What we're seeing now is the Mark he's kept hidden. This obsession of his to get hold of your ranch has only fetched it to the surface. The man's a thorough scoundrel who will scruple at nothing to get what he wants. And what he wants right now is the Circle Dot."

"But *why?*" Those green eyes above her freckles looked almost desperate probing my features. "If I only knew why—what kind of maggot has got into his head, I might—"

"Wouldn't make a bit of difference," I said harshly. "What you don't know ain't like to hurt you. It's the knowing that's dangerous—"

She faced me squarely. "If you know that much you must know what's driving him."

"I might have a crazy suspicion," I said, "but that's as far as it goes, Terry. Honest. What I've latched on to looks just plain impossible."

"Well, I don't see why you can't tell me. If it's my place he's after—and you've already said it *is* the Circle Dot—then I've a right to know why!"

When she looked at me like that I found it uncommonly hard to stick to my resolve, but I knew in my bones the near-incredible thing I believed I had discovered was nothing she could afford to have bruited around. One careless word and we'd have every greedy bastard in the country coming down on us. Bad enough as it was—we could never fight off a horde of Mark Elders.

"I guess you do," I finally admitted, "but I'm not goin' to say another word on the subject."

She turned away from me white-cheeked and I reckoned right then I'd lost any chance I'd ever had of winning her. But a secret shared is no longer a secret. The only thing I could do was to keep my mouth shut. And some way figure how to rid us of Mark.

CHAPTER
33

She said of a sudden, "I suppose you think my decision to run for sheriff is pretty silly."

Well, I did. "If you feel like you want to get into politics far be it from me to discourage you."

"I don't. It's a man's job, of course. I've filed because it seems to me if the current incumbent had the best interests of this country at heart the things Mark's done would have forced him to act. But he's stood back, apparently satisfied to close his eyes to these killings. He has to know Mark ought to be in jail. I realize Mark has a lot of clout around here but—"

"You could get him put under bond to keep the peace," I suggested, knowing of course there'd not be enough teeth in that to stop him. She knew it, too.

"I've not forgotten my mother," she said with her eyes fiercely on me. "Whatever his reason the man's a mad dog!"

"When's the election?"

"Four days from now."

I said, "You've done no campaigning and there's no time for it now." Just the thought of her out in the hustings, exposing herself to Mark's machinations, gave me the jitters. "I think you ought to withdraw from the race."

Her chin came up. She looked mighty determined. "Win or lose I intend to go on with it!" She eyed me defiantly. "He belongs behind bars!"

"Well," I said, "I've got no quarrel with that."

"When you saw what he was up to you should have put in for sheriff yourself."

"Fine sheriff I'd make—"

"If you'd show a little gumption . . ."

So that was what she thought of me! Ignoring the scowl on my face, she said bitterly, "I should think after the way you've been treated . . . are you *afraid* of the man?"

Though I wasn't about to admit that to anyone, she'd put her finger right on what I'd been asking myself. *Was* I afraid of him?

Swinging round on my heel I headed for the day pen and the horses kept up for any sudden emergency. I expect my face was black as thunder. That was certainly how I felt inside. Angry, humiliated, bitterly resentful.

"Wait, Gill, I—"

It was too much to stomach. I roped out a horse, flung on my saddle, gave the critter a taste of my knee, and jerked the trunk strap more savage than need be, wishing by God I had a dog to kick.

Climbing aboard, both feet in the stirrups, I'd no idea of where I was going; I dug in my spurs and rode away from the Circle Dot.

By the time I'd cut loose of my furious thoughts I found myself bound through the hills toward my own place, the horse spread I'd once figured to make me independent. No chance of that now. I was so riled up, so muddled in my head, I never even thought to scout the place first but rode straight in to find a paper tacked to the door.

I'd no need to read it to know what that would be, but piling out of the saddle in another gust of anger I got myself over there to find the proof of my notion set out in black and white. As suspected it was a notice of foreclosure. I ripped it from the door, tore it to shreds and flung it away.

A futile gesture but highly satisfying to my long-bottled urge for destruction.

Standing there, glowering, I whirled, reaching hipward at the cat-footed sound of encroaching boots coming up from behind, squeezing the trigger in my fury before fully seeing the shape of what I was shooting at.

My astonishment was no greater than the startled incredulity puckering Chico's gone-gray face as he crumpled and pitched forward, the knife falling from his hand.

CHAPTER
34

Long moments passed.

I hardly knew what to think of myself as fright, worry, and a crazy exultation followed my amazement in rapid succession. I had killed the killer. All by myself I had killed the killer! Me, Gracious Gill, the mouse from Four Corners!

It didn't matter that I never could have done it had I realized who was back of me. I felt ten feet tall. Vindicated, if you've a mind to call it that. There wasn't an ounce of regret inside me as I stood in my tracks staring down at him.

I left him right where he was and went into the house, not giving a damn who might happen to see him—if the truth be told, hoping somebody would. I had never before killed anybody and was astonished to discover how easy it was. I suppose I was in shock though it never occurred to me. I had enough sense to swab out my gun and replace the spent cartridge, then went over to the mantel and took down the old Sharps buffalo gun that spent most of its time resting on a set of antlers. After that I went outside and sat down on the steps with the loaded Sharps across my lap, ready and waiting for Mark's next hired killer, determined that this one shouldn't even get near me.

Only carrying one shot this gun could knock a man over at four hundred yards. It was no kind of weapon to stamp your boot and yell boo! at.

Rolling up a smoke from my Bull Durham sack I sat there puffing like a frog on a lily pad, pondering now how incredibly lucky I'd been in that matter of Chico. If he'd thrown the knife it seemed reasonably certain I wouldn't be sitting here enjoying the breeze. I found that my hands were shaking a bit and scowled at them fiercely, willing them quiet.

A couple of buzzards were sailing the blue and were only kept off by the sight of my gun. Then I heard the slow clopping of hoofs coming nearer and braced myself for whatever was in store. My hands began to sweat where they gripped the Sharps, and narrowing my eyes against the glare I presently picked out Mark Elder coming up the trail from the flats, surprisingly alone, and was mightily tempted to put a bullet through him.

I got to my feet and knocked the horse out from under him, somewhat chagrined that he hadn't been pinned under it.

"You goddamn fool," he shouted, "what'd you want to do that for?"

"Thought the walk would do you good," I said calmly. "In case you didn't know it you're not welcome around here." I shoved a new load in the rifle. "Start hikin'."

"You're on my property!"

"Says who?"

"Why, damn you," he yelled. "The sheriff served fore-closure papers—"

"I ain't seen no papers. No sheriff, either, an' if you don't start walkin' I'm like to do you a hurt."

I guess seeing me lifting that big old Sharps must have shaken a lot of the wind from his sails. Suddenly he appeared to discover dead Chico. "Pick him up," I said, "and get the hell out of here."

His eyes bugged out. "You gone off your rocker? Did you shoot that feller?"

"You see anyone else around here might have done it? Pick him up," I said, "before I salivate *you!*"

When I put the butt of that big gun against my shoulder he made haste with bitter cursing to settle Chico over a shoulder and go lurching off in the direction from which he'd come.

I watched him out of sight, then walking over to where his dead horse lay I pulled the rifle from his saddle sheath and went back with it to the house. I tell you it done me a heap of good forcing that bastard to lug off his hired bravo. I didn't reckon he would lug Chico far, but at least I'd got the pair of them out of my yard.

It must have made a new man of me; at least I quit worrying about Mark Elder. In this new feeling of well-being I looked through the house I'd put up three years ago, which Mark had figured to have taken away from me, and decided to spend the night in my own bed. The Bar B Cross foreman, Ullbrack, had laid in a good supply of eatables before Bill Hazel had got him out of here.

There was, of course, always the chance of Mark trying to retake it, but unless he had managed to augment his crew I didn't think it likely my sleep would be much disturbed.

Nor was it.

After fixing me some breakfast I decided to go on over to the Circle Dot to pick up any news they might have and, stepping outside, got an unpleasant surprise. Dead Chico was back, sprawled right where I'd dropped him!

• • •

This gave me a nasty turn, no denying it. The likeliest reason for fetching back Chico's cadaver was to give Mark's tame sheriff an excuse to jail me or, more probably, get me hanged on some sort of cooked-up testimony. Mark's own dead horse had not been moved.

I wasted no time trying to sort out his motives but, saddling up, took off through the hills to get back to Terry and my friends at the Circle Dot. It came into my mind that Tolliver, busily sheeping the cow crowd off their range, hadn't followed through with the hands he'd offered to loan the Circle Dot; none of them, anyway, had made themselves manifest. Either it had slipped Tolliver's mind or something had come up to change his thinking though it was obviously possible the offer had never been intended to be kept.

There were now but three days between us and that election and most likely, I reckoned, Terry's three hands and Barbona would be wanting to ride in and vote for her. I disliked the thought of leaving the Circle Dot undefended, but if Mark had picked that time for a raid I doubted I'd be adequate to hold them off and, anyway, Terry would be expecting me to ride in with the others.

Still another unpleasant notion came over me. This had to do with the return of that knifer's cadaver. If it had been put back for Mark's prodded sheriff to have a look at, not finding me there the man would be sure to make tracks for Terry's place—Mark no doubt having already pointed out that with an election right on top of him it behooved the sheriff to improve his image by making a few arrests.

With the sun well up in all its splendor I rode into Terry's yard a few minutes short of nine to find Ace Jolly aboard his horse facing Terry and her crew lined up before the porch.

I caught no change in her expression as I pulled up alongside Jolly. "What's up?" I said, looking round.

Ace Jolly, with smirky smile, declared, "I've ridden over at behest of Mark to put an end to this quarreling. He's offering to buy Miz Terry out—very generous offer, all things considered."

"And I've told him," Terry said, "there's no inducement he could offer that would fine me leaving the Circle Dot."

Mark's courier twisted around in his saddle to put his unctuous eyes on me. "Mark's made a fair offer in the interest of amity. Ten thousand, cash, don't float around ever' day! If you got any influence with this young lady—"

" 'Fraid you're barkin' up the wrong tree with that," I cut in. "She has a mind of her own. If she tells you she's not interested in selling you can believe she means exactly that."

Jolly said with a scowl, "Man can't reason with a bunch of dang fools," then turned his horse and kicked it into a run.

"I thought you'd cleared out," Terry said to me. The look she put on me was cold and hard. "What brings you back?"

"Reckon you know the answer to that."

There was a quick vitality in the way those green eyes skewered into my face. In the quickened way her breast rose and fell I read a glimmer of hope that all was not yet over between us. Stepping away from the porch she came up to my horse, but in her upturned features I found no softening. "What brought you back?"

"I just wanted you to know . . ." Damn it, put in bare words it would sound like boasting!

"Yes?" she said, not giving an inch in the way she looked up at me. "What did you want me to know?"

Those others were watching me, too. Inscrutibly.

"That I think," I said, "if you all ride into Four Corners for that election, by the time you get back you'll find Mark in possession."

"Well . . ." I could see her weighing that, finding it likely. Her eyes came back to me, narrowing. "And were you going to propose settling in here to hold them off?"

"It had crossed my mind."

"Don't put yourself out."

"I didn't figure to," I said, getting back some of the anger I'd ridden away from here with. I didn't know much about women, as you'll have doubtless surmised, but if she was a fair example I reckoned I was better off without one. I was touching my hat, about to turn and ride off, when the sheriff rode up with two helpers, who spread out looking ugly. "I have to arrest you, Gill, for the murder of a Mex'kin I understand is called Chico. I advise you to come along peaceful—"

"What gives you the notion I murdered him?" I asked, ignoring the startled looks focused on me by the Circle Dot contingent.

"Mr. Mark Elder informed me he was there when it happened. That you threw down on the feller without provocation—"

"Mr. Mark Elder was nowhere around when that bugger was killed. What he's fed you is a pack of lies."

"You denyin' you killed that feller?" asked the boss star-packer, ignoring my words.

"I killed him all right, when he snuck up behind figurin' to drive a knife into me."

"We've looked over that ground round the corpse mighty careful. His iron, unfired, was still in his holster. We found no knife—"

"Then you better talk to Elder about that. When I shot him he had a knife in his fist. Had I been an instant slower he'd have had it in me," I told him without embroidery.

Dude Inman said, "That Chico polecat come here two, three days ago claimin' Diego Quintares sent him to give us a hand. Short time he was here he killed two of our Yaquis and a Navajo kid who worked for Gill—all three of 'em knifed. An' every last one of us will swear to it!"

Sheriff didn't seem much interested in that. "He claimed Quintares sent him?"

"That's what he claimed. Quintares denies it. If Gill killed that rat he oughta git a medal for it."

"Yeah," Hazel seconded, "however he done it."

"I have to go by the facts," this pompous rascal said, rubbing a hand across his badge. "Mr. Mark Elder has made a complaint. I have a warrant in my pocket—"

"And I'm swearing out a complaint against Mark Elder," Terry cried, "for shooting my mother to shut her mouth about the things he's done to get hold of this ranch! For trying to force me to marry him and for deliberately smashing Lockhart's gun hand! Show the sheriff your hand, Reb."

Lockhart held up his hook.

The sheriff refused to look. "Mr. Elder's an important man in this country," he said, looking down his nose at Terry. "If you traipse around saying things like that—"

"You callin' her a liar?" Reb Lockhart said, starting toward him.

Watching out for that hook, the sheriff, backing off, forgot all about me. His deputies did, too, so when Bill Hazel grabbed Reb and the sheriff found a chance to fetch his stare back to me, he saw the gun in my hand focused square at his paunch and turned gray as old stone.

"Now see here!" he blustered in a halfhearted fashion, "put away that gun and I'll forget you drawed it. You're in deep enough now without resistin' an officer in performance of his duty. Mr. Elder wouldn't lie—"

I motioned with my gun. "Hit the trail," I said, "an' take your carpetbaggers with you."

CHAPTER
35

He made a last futile stab to recover his lost initiative. "Afraid you'll regret this," he intoned portentiously. "Killin' that poor Mex'kin, resistin' an officer, consortin' with known outlaws, makin' false accusations against a prominent citizen." Shaking his head he let out a sigh. "Reckon I'll be seein' the lot of you behind bars."

Sweeping a glance across the assembled company, seeing the white-knuckled hands clamped to gun butts, he wheeled his mount with a jerk of the head and rode off down the trail that let onto the flats, his two understrappers following.

I saw Terry watching me, an odd look twisting the shape of her mouth. "A lucky shot," I said, "not a whisper too soon," passing it off like an old hand at such things.

She said, "Was Mark really there?"

"He was there, all right, but later. I shot the horse out from under him. Told him to pick up his carrion an' start hikin'. Probably dumped Chico's relic soon's he got out of sight. Must have found some help durin' the night and fetched Chico back again, all carefully placed for that jackass to look at."

Eyes seeming larger, wheeling back to me in that direct way they had, she said in a wondering tone, "I believe you *did* kill that fellow."

I dredged up a wry grin. "Does seem powerful unlikely, don't it? I didn't have much choice." The three men were still staring as though at some freak they had found at a sideshow. "Takes a heap of salt," I said, and then to Terry said, "You folks still feed at noon around here?"

"I'll go fix some sandwiches."

Cowpuncher fixings at this time of day, if you got anything at all, were mostly meat or mostly beans. An El Paso packer for a considerable while had been doing for beans what Arbuckle had done for cowpuncher coffee. He fried and refried them till what you got was a sort of thick paste you could slap between two slabs of bread. This goop came in cans plumb ready to eat, all you added was the bread or biscuits. The quick fix, some called this.

Since few cowhands can be persuaded to eat mutton it was a foregone conclusion we were going to get beans. Despite its volatile nature, this sort of fare stays by you mighty well. I hadn't chomped on much since I'd got my new teeth, but guessed with proper care I could manage one of these.

I took mine back outside. Holding a tin cup of scalding java in my free hand I sat down on the bench below the cookshack window and got gingerly to work. Reb Lockhart joined me. His handicap made mine seem puny, for when it came to shoveling food into your system an iron hook held no advantage.

I've heard a lot of loose talk about the ebulient nature of ranch hands at table. Kidding and horseplay were notably absent from meals at the Circle Dot. Enthusiasm was generally limited to stoking the inner man. I did however on this occasion catch the muffled tag-end of something Bill Hazel had presumably aimed at Terry. Just part of a sentence likening someone to a lightning rod—most probably me. Regretfully I did not catch her reply.

What I had seen on that hogback with her a few days ago, and the near-incredible notion I'd dredged from it, continued bitterly to plague me. My wickedness in keeping from her what I suspected—the value of this asset and the nature of it—had kicked up feelings of guilt not easily brushed aside.

It was entirely true that one careless word, if it reached the wrong ears, could fetch a stampede that would make Sutter's Mill seem a picnic, leaving her with nothing, luring too many roughnecks for us to contend with. But in keeping my suspicions to myself I had been, and still was, activated mainly by what I considered to be my own best interests. I dreaded to obliterate my last chance of winning her.

Through the years I had always had wedding her in mind, an honorable passion I had made no attempt to buttress. My chances, if I'd had any, had never appeared sufficiently robust to put my hope into words. While she was poor and struggling to hold on to her inheritance I'd been foolishly content to lallygag along without airing my desire. Now if I spoke and she knew what I suspected I'd be put in the position of trying to acquire a rich wife.

It wasn't the assets I wanted but her.

It had been a continual struggle to keep my mouth shut. I knew in all fairness I should make known to her my suspicions. I *wanted* to tell her yet couldn't bring myself to. It was a horrible knowledge to lug around day and night, playing hob with my temper.

Sitting there, mouth filled with refried beans, I considered what might happen if I should die without unburdening myself.

I got up off the bench. Passing Hazel and Dude Inman coming out I went into the cookshack to find her sitting at the table, morosely gazing into space, visualizing something so intently she was unaware of my presence. She had beautiful skin despite the freckles boldly showing below the emerald eyes. An outdoor girl who could handle a rope or a bronc with the best of them. She wore country clothes and they suited her, emphasizing the easy grace of her movements. She had full womanly lips needing no aid to nature. Her face was long rather than wide and you could see the character in it, some of the wanting softened by the intelligence with which she appraised all things.

"Terry," I said, "would you consider marrying me?"

CHAPTER
36

Since she sat without movement I thought at first she'd been too caught up in her thinking to hear me. Then with an obvious reluctance her face came round to take me in, and not for the first time I realized she belonged here in the rugged wildness of these tangled hills.

Smiling wryly she said, "Two orphans with scarcely ten dollars between them? You're not serious, are you?"

"Well, I'm no great catch if you're looking for romance. I haven't Piki's flamboyance. I don't have Mark Elder's greedy ambition or the business sense of Diego Quintares. But, yes, I'm serious. Long as we've known each other I've loved you—I'd like to go on loving you the rest of my life." Once again, when I'd got enough spit, I put the question. "Will you marry me?"

"Why the sudden impatience? Have I something you want?"

I would sooner have caught a hoof in the gut. It took every bit of my energy to stand, a target for those probing eyes while I did what I could to find words that made sense. All I could scrape up to say was, "I want you," and had a half moment's fright of what my words might get in return.

I could feel my hopes shrivel under her look of amuse-
ment. "I'm not up for grabs, Gill. Hadn't you better be
thinking about your horses?"

Taking hold of my emotions under that level regard was
not the kind of thing I'd want to go through again. I thought
of what I'd seen on that hogback and told myself there were
other compensations for a man who'd had his eyes opened.
"Expect you're right," I answered shortly and wheeled out
of the place through the coffee smell, striding past the stove
into the increasing glare of the sun and past the stares of
Lockhart and Inman, and got onto my horse and flung him
toward town, hearing Hazel call after me.

To hell with them, I thought in this black surge of fury,
seeing plainly now that if they thought of it at all they considered my engagement with Chico no more than a lucky
fluke. It was, with but two days left before the election, it
was high time I was looking out for Number One.

I rode past my place without even pausing, slamming
my horse down the trail to the flats, still torn up inside
and hunting someone who might offer an outlet for all the
raw notions that churned through my head.

Barreling onto the flats some hour or so later, seeing the
first of Ace Jolly's windmills with Tolliver's sheep thinly
scattered around it, the first stirring of caution began to seep
through the wildness inside me. No walkers, no riders, were
anyplace in sight, and I pushed steadily on, having calmed
enough now to wonder if I'd had the boldness to grab
Terrance O'Brian back there in the cookshack, crushed
her to me in a hungry embrace, might not things have
been different.

I told myself might-have-beens buttered no parsnips.

Passing the burnt-out shells of Jolly's gutted buildings I
pressed on toward Rock Springs and the Bar B Cross line

camp, the scene of my shabby humiliations at the hands of Mark Elder. Bitter memories of that fiasco sharpened my stare and fetched the subsiding anger pounding through my veins again.

I'd long envied those who could take their pleasure, living it to the full with no care for the morrow or attendant consequences. This took confidence, an unquenchable belief in the rightness of self and self's desires, a thing I'd never had. Like Mark, that swashbuckling Barbona had this quality in hateful abundance. If I could pattern myself on Piki I might get somewhere in this miserable world.

Despite the daily give and take of long acquaintance, my own assessment of Terrance O'Brian had set her as far away as the moon. Now, beset on all sides and with even less cash to draw on than myself, I could tell by the remembered look of her face she was still as far out of my reach as she'd ever been. I could see for myself it was my own lack of confidence that had kept me from being any more than I was to her. Face value in this world was what moved mountains, the kind of confidence I'd never latched on to.

An old saw held that timidity of outlook never won a fair lady. I needed to recapture the feeling I'd had after killing that knifer. I resolved to work on it, to give Terrance and others a good look at the fellow who lived inside my rabbity appearance.

With this thought in mind I came upon Tolliver talking with Mexico and one of their Yaquis at Jolly's number-twelve mill. The errand boy's dark cocky features with that jagged scar across the left temple abruptly wheeled to me as I pulled up my horse some three lengths away from them. The man's crippled hand reached out to nudge Tolliver, who came around in his saddle to throw me a negligent stare.

"Howdy, Gill. Guess you can see we're about to take over this end of the cactus. In another couple days you'll not see a cow anywhere on these flats."

"What I don't see is those horses you were going to take care of for me."

He cocked his head to one side and showed his snaggle-toothed grin. "That's right." He laughed. "In my kind of business them broncs could be important. What'll you take for 'em?"

"I'll take them out of your hide if they're not back on my pastures by this time tomorrow."

He peered at me, astonished. "Mexico," he said from the off side of his mouth, "you noticed what a long tail this critter's got?"

With no sign of my apprehensions, I told him flatly, "Watch out it don't slap you. You're lookin' at a man who's not to be trifled with."

"That so?" He took a quick squint around like he wondered where reinforcements were lurking. "Glad you told me, for I'd never have guessed it." Without taking his patronizing look off me he said to his scar-faced dogs-body, "Shove him off that horse. We'll trade him to Elder for—"

The rest was drowned in the bark of my hogleg, another lucky fluke that found his cocky henchman knocked half out of the saddle with cheeks bone-white and crippled hand clamped to a bloody shoulder.

Tolliver grumbled, "You'd no call to do that." His eyes fastened on the smoking snout pointed at him. "Can't you take a little teasin'?"

"I'm all through bein' pushed around," I said. "Even a rat will bite if it's cornered. Now you get those horses headed for my place in one hell of a hustle. Go on—git whackin'!"

● ● ●

Watching those two till they were well out of rifle range I'd no confidence at all that they would go on and do it, but at least they'd discovered I'd strike back if I had to. And striking back right then was looming large in my thinking. I didn't figure shocked surprise would carry me through many more of these encounters, but I'd broken anyway through the paralysis of caution. Once the word got around that I could give as well as take, a few of these machos might step a mite more careful.

Made me feel a heap better as I began my hunt for Mark.

I spent the rest of the day at it, part of the night and all the next morning, without once sighting either Mark or his roughnecks. It was during the middle of this second afternoon when it came over me that the most likely place to find them was at my abandoned spread, that eight hundred acres I had had such bright hopes for.

At this point in time I was only some four of five miles away. So, leaving the flats, I put my mount on the trail climbing east through those rolling hills with the blue mountain crags looming distantly over their tops.

Perhaps I owed it to myself, I thought, to make another try at showing Terry there was more to me than she had so far seen and not give up like a beaten dog.

The feel of the sun on my back was right warm despite the breeze coursing through these troughs, and the smell of resin coming out of the dusty head-high brush seemed to put new life in me. This was *my* country for as long as I could hold it, and I told myself I was not whipped yet.

Tomorrow was the day of the big election and, though it might be a foolhardy thing to do, I intended to be in Four Corners whether I rode with Terry or not.

CHAPTER
37

Just as I was about to come in sight of my place, where it lay spread out to the left of the trail going on through the hills to the Circle Dot, the sudden nicker of a horse had me grabbing the Sharps out from under my leg. Not waiting for an answer the unseen horse let out an excited whinny, and with the Sharps up and ready I took the last turn at a spur-induced run.

No two-legged varmints anywhere in sight. What I did see straightoff was old Surefoot standing there whinnying and tossing his head, trying to get free of the leadshank that held him hitched to the front gate. And off in the corrals beyond the fence I saw most of my horses, heads up and nickering. Whatever the reason I was back in business.

I did not imagine I'd thrown a scare into Tolliver. He was not the kind you could scare that easy. I turned the horse I'd been riding into one of the fenced pastures and was packing my gear to put it back on Surefoot when Bill Hazel rode up and stopped outside the gate. "Got your horses back, have you? Didn't reckon you'd see hide nor hair of 'em again."

"Wants to stay on the good side of me, I guess." Actually I didn't believe the sheepman gave a damn for my opinion.

He'd given back my horses because his calculated purpose in going onto those flats with his sheep had been to find feed. If pushing out the cows didn't cost him a lot he took pleasure in doing it. Any feud with us hill men might prove a dangerous distraction. This, I figured, was why I'd got my horses back. Tolliver had no hankering to be caught between two fires.

I did not feel obligated to explain this to Hazel. He said, "I've come over to find out if you're riding in with us tomorrow."

"Don't look very likely."

I could feel his stare while I was getting old Surefoot ready to travel.

"Goin' to vote, ain't you?"

"If I have time," I said, giving a yank on the trunk strap. I could feel his stare digging into me harder. "I'm not one of Miz Terry's hands. Happens I've got business of my own needs tendin'."

He heeled his mount back into the trail with a disgusted snort. "Some friends," he growled, "a man is better off without."

"That's the way I look at it."

I sent a few forkfuls of hay over the bars, made sure the troughs held water and went into the house for a last look around. I wasn't happy to be leaving this place open to vandals. Everything in it held a heap of memories, not to mention aspirations. I thrust some fodder for the Sharps into one of my pockets, put on my nighttime hat, tramped out and climbed into the saddle.

I reckoned I ought to been hungry but wasn't. I felt no great hurry about getting there. Polls wouldn't open before seven o'clock. Seemed like all the hours of my life since Mark had thrown aside his mask and brutally killed

Terry's mother had been pushing me toward this inevitable confrontation.

In the deepening dusk with bullbats swooping after night-flying moths the stage road to Four Corners looked silver gray as I dawdled along, not caring to arrive there before mid-morning, the good feeling of Surefoot between my legs evoking old memories of things long past, church box suppers and schoolhouse dances.

I'd no doubt at all but that Mark would be there. Shoved off his own range by Tolliver's sheep, cattle scattered and not over three hands he could still depend on, it seemed plain he'd be in his most dangerous mood. Wild at seeing his gains stripped from him, his sheriff in danger of losing his job, probably worried lest Quintares be drawn into this, he'd be desperate to make the Circle Dot his own. I guessed he understood now that even if he took it he could not hang on to it without Terry to clinch his title.

If she won this election he could be in a bad way.

It was a little past nine when I rode into Four Corners.

A lot of rigs and horses lined both sides of the street. I watered Surefoot, put him up at a livery, went into the Last Chance hash house and got me some breakfast, then went into a bar and had a short beer.

Still carrying my Sharps and keeping my eyes peeled, I hunted up the polling place and reluctantly joined the line outside. A man with a badge came up to me. "No weapons allowed in the polling place, Mac."

After eyeing him a moment I stepped out of line. One vote more or less wasn't going to effect Terry. A ballot was tacked up outside the entrance, and lacking anything better to do I walked over to have a look at it, astonished to discover Terry's name wasn't on it.

I saw a man with pale eyes crouched on his boot heels beneath a low-crowned hat some thirty feet away with his back against the schoolhouse wall. There was another hunkered down outside the mercantile making little pictures in the dust with a pointed stick. I saw Dude Inman then coming out of the saloon next door. I caught his eye and he came over.

"Bad smell in this town," he muttered, joining me. "Reckon you've noticed Terry's not on the ballot."

I nodded. "Been wonderin' how come."

He said, "She's trying to find out."

"Barbona ride in with you?"

"No. But he's around here someplace. All the law in town is quartered round the schoolhouse. Sheriff's inside tryin' to charm the voters."

"With no competition I wouldn't think he'd bother."

"Folks can write her name in." His eyes skittered round like a nervous bronc's. "That's what we done. Hazel's down at the other end of town tryin' to rally up some write-ins."

"Where's Reb?"

"He went with Terry. Over to the courthouse."

"Let's look around some more."

He fell in with my suggestion and we meandered round looking over the crowded walks, the gesticulating gabbers, discovering three or four more idle squatters hunkered in such shade as the few trees afforded. I seemed to sense a pattern in the way these lone idlers were positioned but, recognizing none of them, I'd no way of knowing what outfit they belonged to. All of Quintares' hands were big-hatted Mexicans or Yaquis, and we did see a few who might be on the Villalobos payroll.

Several Cornish miners were occasionally visible among the shifting throngs. I did not see any obvious sheepmen.

Dude said he'd not seen any either, nor anyone recognizable as coming from the Bar B Cross. "Have you seen Mark?" I asked, and he said he hadn't, though he thought it possible Mark had taken on a few hardcases to augment what was left of his crew. I said, "Let's go see if Terry's still at the courthouse."

If she was we failed to discover her, though we spent half an hour meandering up and down its halls, opening closed doors and backing hurriedly out again. We finally latched on to a man who suspected he had seen her going off with some ranny maybe twenty minutes ago. "That the dame who was figurin' to run for sheriff?"

Dude nodded. I said, "Anything odd about the man you think she went off with?"

"Well, he had a hand on the right arm and a hook on the left."

"You see which way they went?"

"Never noticed. Sorry."

Having thanked him, Dude said, "We won't find her here. Maybe we better get back on the street."

As we did so a bunch of skallyhooting horsemen in big sombreros and tight-fitting pants came larruping along the middle of the road, kicking up dust and yelling their heads off. Dude, looking scornful, said, "Some of Quintares' outfit. What I need's a good stiff drink."

"See you later then," I said, and went off to get my horse. When I came back aboard Surefoot I found Dude waiting out in front of the courthouse on one of the Circle Dot horses. "See a lot more from the back of a horse," he observed, and I nodded.

"Make a better target," I said, looking round. "I'll stay on the street. You go around to the back ends of these alleys."

"What are we lookin' for?"

"Lockhart."

That fetched his head around sharply. "You think they've run into trouble?" I brought the Sharps up across my lap. "Let's find out."

It was Dude that found Reb, dead with a knife buried back of his wishbone.

CHAPTER
38

The shotgun, unfired, lay where his dying fingers had dropped it. I got a blind off the nearest window and we carried Lockhart across to the courthouse and left him, blind and all, on a table in the U.S. Attorney's office with a note hastily scrawled on his official stationery: VICTIM OF A VARMINT UNDER SHERIFF'S PROTECTION. I signed my name to it and fastened it onto the haft of the knife, vindictively thinking what an uproar it might fetch if read by others before the Big Man saw it.

"You recollect," I said, "the way that fake vaquero Chico, did away with three of the boys on our side?" When Inman nodded, I told him I reckoned this was more of the same, that we could expect most anytime to come onto another relic.

There was something uneasy in the slant of Dude's stare. "You mean another of Miz Terry's hands—another *corpse?*"

"That's the way I see it. Mark's got two choices. Simplest is to keep whittlin' away at us, pickin' off her supporters one at a time."

"Maybe I better find Hazel an' warn him . . ."

Under less stringent circumstances Dude's alarm would

have been really humorous. But the way things were I reckoned nothing was like to pull a laugh out of me. I said reluctantly, "Maybe you had," and watched for a moment as he
headed uptown. By the time he got out of sight, I thought,
he'd be scratching that horse like a bronc-stomper.

It was hard not to cuss when you toted up the players.
You could count Terry's help on two fingers now. Bill
Hazel and myself. That was how I saw it. And I didn't
know where she was.

I reckoned it was time I did some serious looking.

Where to start was the question.

I guessed the other end of town, and with the Sharps
cradled ready across my lap I kneed Surefoot forward at
his most circumspect pace, being in no hurry to get myself
killed.

Durty Doris' place was off to the right of me, the gun
shop next to it. Sitting up there in Surefoot's saddle was
like riding through a fishbowl, I reckoned with a grimace;
made me feel purely naked.

I passed the hoof-shaper's place, the smell of its forge
hanging sharp in the still air. Less than an hour ago there'd
been rigs and people everywhere you looked. The rigs
were still there, but round here anyway all the quick had
departed; folks brought up on trouble knew when to hunt
a hole.

I kept Surefoot, watchful, to the middle of the road where
I could keep tabs on both sides, not forgetting the roofs,
which in Four Corners were for the most part flat, though
front walls generally rose a foot or so above them, good
protection for a sniper with a rifle.

The Ajax Saloon lay just ahead of me now and I remembered the way I'd larruped past it with Piki Barbona the
night I'd visited that tooth mauler.

The bright smash of afternoon's sun lay against it now picking out the sandblasted look of faded letters. And it was there that I saw on its steps the sprawled shape of Bill Hazel in his spreading gore, trying to get up and knowing he'd never make it.

"Gill," he croaked, "they've got your girl . . ."

Cattycornered from those steps beyond the street's opposite walk was the narrow shape of a private dwelling, its door painted blue in some far-off time and decorated now by holes left by bullets, mute evidence of cowpunchers in for a once-a-month spree.

Nearing this, back to my left between hitched horses I discovered the crouched shape of Mark Elder grinning at me over a lifting Winchester. Coinciding too exactly with this bitter sight a shout rang out, punctuated by a woman's thin scream. The blue door bulged open in a rush of booted feet and Terry plunged from the house, Ace Jolly in hot pursuit.

Even as I squeezed the trigger and saw Ace knocked yelling against the wall, I realized without thought the whole scene had been rigged to trap me with a now-empty rifle.

I flung it at Mark, deflecting his aim as I left the saddle in a flying leap that fell short two yards of getting my hands on him and, rolling, went under a pitching terrified horse as muzzle flame lashed twice more in my direction.

Ignoring the peril of thrashing hoofs I brought up my pistol, coming onto an elbow and trying through a blur of dancing hoofs to discover where that devil had got to.

A rifle's sharp crack pulled my head around to catch the glint of his weapon and give me a target. I did not hurry that shot but took my time, and was rewarded by seeing the jerk of his shape, and fired again square into his face. I was still there, exultantly staring, when a monstrous hoof blotted everything from sight.

• • •

Next time I took stock of my surroundings I was in bed in a room with a hospital smell that had pink rambler roses climbing up the wallpaper. Terry, with an open book in her lap, was watching me with a probing expression.

"You all right?" I said. "What am I doin' here?"

"You've got a smashed collarbone compliments of that horse."

"Won't keep me from gettin' leg-shackled will it?"

The queerest look came over her face. "I'd no idea you were fixing to get married . . . Who's the girl? Do I know her?"

"If you'd bend this way a couple more inches I could touch her."

Startled eyes opened wide. "Aren't you taking rather a lot for granted?"

I said, "If you're not interested, what are you doing here?"

"Well, somebody had to look after you."

I hadn't realized a man could feel so weak. But I kept doggedly at it. "Now that you're about to become a rich female, you're the one who's goin' to need looking after."

"So you *did* see something up on that hogback! What was it?" she demanded, leaning a mite closer.

"Same thing you did. Only difference is you thought that black goo was coming from a dyin' saguaro, whereas I'll give odds it was coming from an oil seep. Now let's quit sparrin'. You going to marry me or ain't you?"

Hearing the laugh that fetched out of her I could see what a fool I'd been ever to imagine this could end any different. But then she took my breath away.

"You didn't think that would put me off, did you?"